THE
MIDWIFE

BOOKS BY VICTORIA JENKINS

The Divorce

The Argument

The Accusation

The Playdate

The New Family

The Bridesmaids

DETECTIVES KING AND LANE SERIES

The Girls in the Water

The First One to Die

Nobody's Child

A Promise to the Dead

THE
MIDWIFE

VICTORIA
JENKINS

bookouture

Published by Bookouture in 2022

An imprint of Storyfire Ltd.
Carmelite House
50 Victoria Embankment
London EC4Y 0DZ

www.bookouture.com

ISBN: 978-1-80314-865-6
eBook ISBN: 978-1-80314-864-9

PROLOGUE

The woman and the girl sat together on the sofa in the living room, the lighting muted to just the lamp on the side table, the late night shut out by the closed curtains. The girl was curled into her, her head resting against the woman's stomach. She didn't seem capable of crying. Something had been switched off, a fuse short-circuited that had dried up her tears. Instead, she sat motionless, her body coiled like a cat's, quietly absorbing the caresses of the woman's fingers against her fine hair. The woman didn't say much; she didn't know what to say. The girl would speak when she was ready.

The question seemed to come from nowhere, when the truth was that it had probably been carried within her for weeks.

'What's a guardian angel?'

The words pierced the woman's heart. She stroked the young girl's dark hair, her eyes moving to the ceiling as she sought the right answer. 'It's an angel who looks after someone, who protects them. You can't see them, but you can feel them there sometimes, when you need them most.'

The room was bathed in silence for a moment as the answer was absorbed.

'Like you, then. Are you my guardian angel?'

The woman smiled sadly. If only that could be true, she thought. 'But you can see me, my darling. And you can see me whenever you need me, okay?'

'Okay.'

Silence persisted, an uninvited third party.

'Can I sleep here again tonight?'

'Of course you can.'

'And you'll look after me? For ever?'

The woman closed her arm around the child, holding her closer. She was asking her for a commitment that was impossible to deliver. 'Nothing will ever hurt you again,' she said. 'I'll make sure of that.'

ONE

THE MOTHER

It seemed strange to Lauren that she should feel alone now, and yet she felt it acutely, this suffocating sense of being separate from the rest of the room. The waiting area was filled with couples, some holding hands, others absent-mindedly scrolling their phones. She could see only one other single woman. Her partner was probably at work, she thought, unable to get the time off to come to the session. Despite not being present that day, he existed.

She watched the young woman thumb through the pages of the folder in her lap, as though able to decipher the charts and scrawled notes kept inside. Lauren had got as far as working out her child's growth chart – a steady line that moved progressively upwards with each check-up – but much of the rest was like reading a foreign language. The young woman closed the folder and looked up as an older woman – not much older than Lauren – approached. A smile passed between them as the older woman sat next to the younger before moving a hand to her arm and giving her sleeve a gentle rub. Her mother, Lauren thought, the realisation a punch to her gut. She had her mother with her.

Lauren had gone through the process of getting pregnant

alone, pouring the majority of her savings into IVF treatment using a donor. She had attended appointments, scans and check-ups without so much as a friend beside her for moral support, yet she had never felt lonely in the way she did this morning. There had been nerves, anticipation, doubt, but until now there had never been this overwhelming sense of isolation.

As she sat clutching her folder of notes and waiting for the session to start, she observed the other people in the room as subtly as she was able, giving sidelong glances of assessment. She was without doubt the oldest expectant mother in the room, which perhaps added to her sense of alienation.

Beside the water dispenser sat a girl who couldn't have been older than twenty-two, bump barely apparent, still able to fit into her skinny jeans. Next to her, a gangly young man of a similar age gazed pale-faced at a poster of a breastfeeding baby, his eyes wide at the realisation of what his future now held. He would be there for the birth, Lauren thought, and the notion struck her with such unexpected clarity that she felt her eyes begin to fill with uncharacteristic tears.

She hastily wiped her eyes with her sleeve, self-conscious and embarrassed. She was grateful for the distraction when one of the midwives who'd been chatting at the reception desk came over to speak to the waiting room.

'Good morning, everyone. Lovely to see you all here today. My name's Sandra Mayhew, I'm one of the midwives here. I'm going to start the session by talking you through the latent phase of labour, labour itself, what you can expect on the day of your delivery, as well as the pain options that will be available to you. There's a lot to take in, so there'll be a chance later to ask me any questions you might have before we have a tour of the birthing centre. Okay, so let's start with what's meant by the latent phase.'

As Sandra spoke, Lauren felt her mind drift. The room seemed too crowded; she felt claustrophobic, and the baby was shifting as though sensing her unease. It had kept her awake for much of the previous night, a clear pattern appearing. If recent weeks were anything to go by, she was bracing herself to be up between the hours of 2 and 4 a.m., which currently seemed to be her unborn child's chosen playtime.

Sandra Mayhew was talking about contractions, but Lauren wasn't sure exactly what had been said. The water dispenser was calling to her, her throat suddenly dry, but she didn't want to get up and cross the room while the midwife was in the middle of addressing the group.

Sandra spoke for another ten minutes before Lauren had an opportunity to get a drink. The rest of the group followed the midwife along the corridor, where Lauren caught up with them. Everyone stood in awkward clusters, boyfriends and husbands nervously eyeing the delivery rooms further ahead.

'Is anyone here considering a water birth?' Sandra asked. Only one woman raised a hand, prompting Sandra into a speech about the benefits of giving birth in one of the unit's new birthing pools. Lauren half listened. Despite the claims that water helped reduce the pain of childbirth, she couldn't think of anything worse. Someone asked a question about the set of scales resting on a nearby trolley. The conversation had gone off on a tangent, and how they'd ended up on the subject of weight, Lauren wasn't sure. Her mind drifted again, this time distracted by the rack of leaflets on the wall beside her. *Healthy eating during pregnancy. Breastfeeding and its benefits. When your baby dies before birth.* That leaflet froze her. It seemed cruel to have it among the others, as part of the same display. Her hand moved to the rack as though separate from the rest of her, and she took one of the leaflets. Its words seemed to bellow at her before blurring into a fine mist.

'Are you okay?'

She turned sharply towards the voice that came from

behind her. The middle-aged woman standing close by gave her a smile, her features soft and friendly.

'Sorry,' she said. 'I didn't mean to make you jump.'

Lauren shook herself from her thoughts. 'I was miles away.'

'I could see that.' The woman glanced at the leaflet. 'First baby?'

Lauren nodded.

'It's daunting for everyone. Even those who don't show it.' The woman offered a second smile. 'My name's Jackie. I'm a midwife. Off duty,' she explained, gesturing to her jeans. 'Just had to pop in to pick something up.' She took the leaflet from Lauren's hand and met her eye, her lips curled into a smile that was at once both kind and pitying. 'Everything's going to be fine.'

'I know,' Lauren said, forcing a smile. She glanced at the group of people ahead of her and felt herself surrounded by youth. 'It's just the whole geriatric mother thing, you know?'

Jackie put a hand on her arm. 'Plenty of women much older than you have delivered healthy babies.' She nodded at the last members of the group, who were following Sandra into one of the delivery suites. 'You'd better catch them up. She'll give you a tour of the birthing rooms next.'

'Okay. Thank you. Hope to see you at the next session.'

'I'll make sure of it.'

TWO

THE MIDWIFE

Jackie turned on her side and rested a hand on Peter's bare chest. The light from the en suite bathroom spilled a muted pool onto the fading hotel carpet, the far side of the room cast into shadow. He turned his head to look at her, his eyes heavy with tiredness. She wondered when he'd last had a full night's sleep that hadn't been interrupted either by a phone call or by his overactive mind. Peter seemed to function on a recipe of caffeine, adrenaline and determination. Time with her might have been a chance for him to switch off for a while, though the purpose of these recent meetings had put a stop to any thought of that.

They had been here many times before over the years, similar generic chain hotels or cheap B and Bs dotted across various parts of the country, circumstances separating them before life found a way of bringing them back together again. This time, it had been Peter's doing. He had contacted her eight months earlier, his voice instantly recognisable though it had been over a decade since they had last seen each other. He had changed so much in that time, more than she had anticipated, but then of course so had she. And yet his body remained familiar. A safe place.

He was ten years older than she was, but to look at him no one would have known he was nearly sixty-five. He kept fit and active, as he had been all his life – his mind and body finely tuned by the nature of his work.

'You okay?' he asked, seeming to sense the uncertainty of her thoughts. 'No regrets?'

'I'm old enough now to know the pointlessness of those.'

The truth was that Jackie had plenty of regrets, but he already knew what they were.

He rolled onto his side and pushed her hair behind her ear. His dark eyes focused on hers, and for a moment Jackie felt under scrutiny. Being here with him was like going back thirty years: she was young again, so much time and possibility ahead of her. Yet she knew it was only an idealised version of their past. The truth was, she had felt this way before, as though everything she said and did was under assessment. Their history was more complicated than anyone realised, only the two of them aware of the ties that bound them.

'You've hardly changed a bit in thirty years, you know that?'

'You don't need to compliment me, Pete. I've already agreed to everything, haven't I?'

He frowned. 'Is that how you see it? A business arrangement?'

She pushed herself up and rearranged the pillows behind her, holding the duvet to her chest, suddenly self-conscious. 'What do *you* see it as?'

'You've always done that,' he said. 'Answered a question with a question.'

'Then you were expecting it, weren't you?' She smiled, though there was little to be happy about. What he had asked of her – the reason she was here with him today – was monumental, the possible repercussions so damning she couldn't bear to linger on them.

Peter leaned over the side of the bed to retrieve the shirt abandoned there. 'Did you meet her today?' he asked, pulling it over his head.

'Yes, I met her.'

'She thinks you already work at the unit?'

Jackie nodded.

'When do you start there?'

'Next week.'

He sighed, a deep exhalation of relief that might have suggested their problems were over. The transfer to Pinewood Hospital had taken longer than either of them had expected it to, but Lauren was still only thirty weeks pregnant. There was still time. But perhaps time wasn't enough. They were both aware of the uncertainty that lay ahead of them. 'Thank you.'

'Look,' Jackie said. 'Don't take this the wrong way, but I'm not doing this for you.'

'Still... I realise how much I'm asking.'

He studied her, the concentration on his face so intense that for a moment Jackie felt uncomfortable beneath his gaze. They knew each other so well, and yet she realised that neither of them really knew anything. The fact remained that Peter could have ended everything for her – she was always aware of that. All those years ago, just a few words from him would have stamped a full stop on her career before it had barely had a chance to begin.

'How does she seem?' he asked.

'Fine. Normal. No one would ever know.' She shook her head. 'How does anyone live a lie like that?'

Peter's eyes met hers, but he said nothing. He didn't need to. She realised the irony. In so many ways, she too had been living a lie. Wasn't everyone, in one way or another?

'You can change your mind,' he said.

Jackie raised an eyebrow. Backing out now wasn't an option. She had gone through everything a hundred times, deliberating over everything that could go wrong, allowing her mind to take her to the most extreme scenarios. Only one outcome was possible. 'If that woman is everything you say she is, I don't really have a choice, do I?'

'If?' he repeated. 'Listen, Jackie. I have never been more certain of anything in my life. That woman is dangerous. I know what she did. I know what's she's capable of doing. If there was any other way of going about this, I'd take it, but we don't have time on our side.'

Jackie pushed her head back into the pillow and closed her eyes.

Peter's hand slipped beneath the duvet, his skin cold against hers as he found her fingers. 'I'm sorry.'

Jackie moved her hand away, embarrassed by a show of affection that was uncharacteristic for him and for them. 'You've never needed to apologise. Let's just do what we have to do.'

THREE

THE MOTHER

Lauren lived in Palmers Green, in a ground-floor flat in a row of Victorian terraced houses. She rented the place from a couple of property developer brothers who she suspected made more money in a month than she earned in a year as a PA, but they were good landlords, always available whenever there was a problem, and she was grateful that she had found somewhere affordable and not too far from the city.

Until the age of thirty-three, she had house-shared in various places in the south-east. Once past thirty, she'd noticed everyone else staying young while she was getting older, and had felt a pressure to get a place of her own now she was no longer a part of the late nights and parties that shaped her housemates' weekends. Living alone these past eight years had been worth the expense, the solitude suiting her well, and she had resolved to keep her life as simple as possible, following an organised routine that she rarely strayed from.

But then there had been Callum. It had been good, for a while. Better than good. She had immersed herself in the comfort of everyday normality: long walks on wet days, longer lunches in the cafés that dotted the high street; evenings spent curled on the sofa together watching films that neither of them would remember the details of because they had talked through them. It was comfortable and safe and good, but none of those things could be permanent when they were built upon a lie.

She went to the kitchen to make a cup of tea. As she stood in the doorway, she watched the ghosts of their past play out in front of her.

'Why don't we make this more official?' Callum had said one evening as he stood at the kettle, waiting for it to boil.

For one awful moment Lauren had thought he was about to propose. She had felt herself grow instantly hot, a thin band of sweat forming at the back of her neck, her heartbeat growing erratic beneath her dress. Grateful when his hand didn't reach for a pocket and no ring box was produced as though from thin air, she'd asked, 'What do you mean?'

'We should move in together, what do you reckon? I'm here most of the time anyway – seems daft us paying two lots of rent.'

'Okay. Romantic. You want to move in to save money?'

Callum rolled his eyes. 'That wasn't what I said. And since when were you into romance anyway? Didn't you once say that grand romantic gestures were usually a cover-up for something?'

She had stalled for a while, putting him off with the practicalities of space and his workplace being across the other side of London, but he had remained persuasive and she had eventually agreed. It was what she'd always wanted, but then talk of children began to filter into the everyday conversations about whose turn it was to put the bins out and what was for tea that evening, and she had felt herself flinch from the subject, trying to avoid it until there had been nowhere left to hide.

Saddened by the memory, she went back into the living room, no longer wanting the tea she had gone to the kitchen to make, and turned on the television. There was nothing she wanted to watch, but she needed to block out the noise of her own thoughts, and at least the sound of the baking contest that was playing out on the screen would offer some distraction from the ghosts of the past.

At just after ten, she fell asleep on the sofa. This over-whelming tiredness kept catching her off guard; she found herself full of energy one moment, ready for bed the next. She had expected the exhaustion that had hit her during the first trimester to become a thing of the past, but as she'd got bigger, it had made a return, and she sometimes felt as though she was dragging herself through the day, moving alongside the motions of life while counting down the weeks to her due date. With the television still on, its sound lowered to a soft murmur in the otherwise silent room, she slept a dreamless and brief sleep.

The shattering of glass woke her. In the darkness, she fumbled for the lamp on the side table, heart pounding as the baby shifted inside her. A pool of soft light was cast across the rug, revealing the chunks of glass that had sprayed across the living room floor. There were some at the end of the sofa, just inches from where she had been curled. The right-hand window had a gaping hole, from which it splintered into an intricate web of cracks. When Lauren scanned the floor, she saw a house brick resting at the bottom of the sideboard.

She picked up the brick. A piece of white paper was folded around it, held in place by an elastic band. With quivering hands, she pulled off the band and unfolded the paper. She was greeted with a single statement, printed in large red letters.

YOU CAN'T RUN FOR EVER.

FOUR

THE MIDWIFE

At 7.10 a.m., and with her twelve-hour shift just ended, Jackie went up to the ward to visit the new mother whose baby she had helped deliver in the early hours of that morning. The woman had been induced the previous day and kept in overnight, and her waters had broken when she'd got up to use the toilet, much to the shock of the fellow expectant mother who'd been holding the bathroom door open for her at the time.

'How are you both doing?' she asked with a smile as she peered into the wheeled cot at the bedside. The baby was sleeping soundly, her tiny hands curled into fists at either side of her head. She was wearing a white sleepsuit dotted with little yellow ducks, and the blanket that lay across her legs gave off a smell of floral fabric conditioner, everything new and fresh and hopeful.

'We're okay. Thanks again for everything.'

'Just doing my job.' As she gazed at the sleeping newborn, her heart tugged with the same wrench she had felt on so many occasions. 'Look at her. She's perfect.' She smiled at the child's mother and shook herself from her reverie. 'I got you this.' She reached into her pocket and took out a Snickers bar, waving it like a magician who'd just pulled a rabbit from a hat. She knew the young mum hadn't eaten anything since the previous day other than a plate of soggy white toast, though after so long without food, it had probably tasted like the best thing she'd ever had.

The woman laughed. 'Where did you find that?'

Jackie had tried to keep her distracted during the labour, their conversation moving from work to friends to food. Through the pain and the intake of gas and air, the young woman had shared details of what she'd described as the best meal she'd ever had, in a tiny bistro on a small Parisian side street during a trip there with her boyfriend just before they'd got engaged. The memory of that day had helped to momentarily remove her from her pain, though what she really wanted more than anything, she'd told Jackie, was a Snickers bar.

'Vending machine near the X-ray unit,' Jackie told her. 'It was the last one.'

The woman smiled as she took it from her. 'You're so kind.'

Jackie returned the smile but made no reply. It was exactly what she hoped other people would think of her, there under the guise of being good and honest.

'I'll leave you to enjoy it in peace. Have it now before the baby wakes and wants a feed.'

She went to the staff room to collect her things before she signed off from her shift. She was tired and couldn't wait to leave work. There was no one else in the staff room, but the computer at the desk in the corner was turned on, its lit screen beckoning her. She sat down and tapped in her login details, using them to access the patient database, then typed the name Lauren Coleman into the search bar before accessing her personal details. There was no pen on the table, so she went to the locker to retrieve her bag.

Sandra entered the room holding her mobile to her ear. Jackie glanced anxiously at the computer screen.

'On hold,' Sandra said, covering the mouthpiece. 'You can never talk to a human being any more, can you?'

Jackie wondered whether that was such a bad thing. Some days, the thought of never having to speak to another person again seemed an attractive prospect. She hurried back to the computer and turned the monitor to hide the screen. As Sandra rummaged about in her coat pocket, her phone wedged between her ear and her shoulder, Jackie scribbled Lauren Coleman's mobile number on a scrap of paper before logging out of the database.

'How's everything going?' Sandra asked. 'Like it here so far?'

The phrasing sounded almost ominous, as though with enough time there would be plenty not to like about the place.

'Yes,' Jackie said, as she stood and went back to her locker. 'All good so far.'

'It's a decent team here. Pressure's easier to cope with when you've got supportive people around you. What made you transfer?'

Jackie pulled her jacket over her uniform. She'd been planning to get changed before she left the hospital, but now she just wanted to get out.

'Oh, you know. Just fancied a change.'

Sandra smiled, but there was something behind her eyes that suggested she didn't believe her. Did she know something? Jackie wondered. But that was impossible.

'I wanted to ask...' Sandra raised a hand, her question cut short by someone answering at the other end of her call. 'Sorry,' she mouthed. 'Hi, yes, I need to speak to someone about a claim on my insurance policy.'

Jackie hastily gathered her belongings and left the room, grateful that Sandra had been distracted. Had she seen her copy out Lauren's phone number? It didn't make sense that Sandra was questioning her now, not when she'd first met her weeks ago. If there'd been things she needed to know when Jackie had started at the hospital, she'd had plenty of opportunity to find out.

You're being paranoid, she told herself. She had an exemplary record, unblemished. Her references shone. Any suspicions would only be prompted by her own behaviour. She stopped outside the automatic doors at the hospital's front entrance and breathed in a deep lungful of fresh air. You can do this, she told herself. You're already doing it.

FIVE

THE MOTHER

In the early hours of the following morning, Lauren stood at the kitchen sink and burned the note that had been wrapped around the brick, the words reduced to ash and washed down the plughole. She felt exhausted, but fear was now also starting to settle in her gut.

The couple who lived in the flat upstairs had been woken by the noise and the man had come downstairs to see what had happened and check that Lauren was okay. They'd lived in the same building for years, yet few words had previously passed between them. Strange, she thought, that it had taken some-thing like this for them to exchange more than a passing nod of acknowledgement, but it was consistent with her experience of London, one of the many things she loved about the place. Anonymity was easy to achieve.

Now, alone at the sink, she wished there was someone she could call to come over, if only to provide another presence in the flat. Adrenaline raced through her, and despite the place now being chilled by the breeze that escaped past the edges of the cardboard box she had flattened out and taped across the hole in the window, she felt hot in her pyjamas, her body fired with a nervous energy that had stayed with her through the early hours of the morning. She hadn't gone to bed, not wanting to leave the living room while the flat wasn't secure, and so she had stayed on the sofa and barely slept, allowing her mind to race to its darkest corners, envisioning things that kept her body tensed and her mind wired in case the worst should happen.

She wasn't expected at the office that day, which she was grateful for. Her boss had suggested that once she reached the thirty-week mark she work a day a week from home, and Lauren had been more than happy to take up the offer. She would have to call someone to get a new window pane fitted. She'd only recently paid for a cot and a pram, so she wasn't sure where the money would come from. She had no idea how much it would cost to have the glass replaced. She was going to have to contact the landlords and tell them what had happened, though how was she going to explain the brick?

You can't run for ever. The words taunted her, whispered on repeat in the silence.

While waiting for morning to break, hoping that daylight would chase away the shadows, Lauren cleaned. She scrubbed the bath and dusted, emptied the fridge to clean its shelves while she tried to empty her mind. By the time the sun had risen, the flat was spotless, though she had yet to return to the living room and see to the shattered glass that still lay strewn across the laminate flooring and the rug. When she finally went back into the room at gone 8 a.m., she took the brick with her and stood at the window, imagining who might have been on the pavement outside her home just hours earlier.

Half an hour later, she called her landlord. 'Karim? It's Lauren Coleman, from Belvedere Road.'

'Hi, Lauren, how are things? Everything all right?'

'Fine, thanks,' she said casually, the words tripping off her tongue in an automatic response. 'I mean... no, not really. Look, the front window was broken last night. I'll get it sorted out today, but I just thought I should let you know.'

'Okay. What happened? Are you all right?'

'Yeah, I'm fine.' But she heard the crack in her voice, and he must have heard it too.

'Will you be in today?' he asked. 'I'll be round that way later, I could come and take a look.'

'I can sort it, it's no problem, I don't want to put you out.'

'You're not. I'll be over just before lunch, that okay?'

For the rest of the morning, Lauren moved through the motions of appearing to work, too distracted to deal with anything more than emails that wouldn't wait until the following day. It was a mistake, she kept telling herself. A coincidence. The brick had been intended for someone else; the wrong flat had been targeted.

As soon as he'd ended their call, she'd regretted phoning Karim. She could have replaced the window pane without him ever having to know it had been broken, but now she'd need to find explanations and excuses. She was going to have to tell yet more lies.

Karim arrived at midday. Wherever he'd been before coming to the flat, it seemed to have involved a building site; his black hair was peppered with dust and he was casually dressed in boots and work gear, a far cry from the suit-clad businessman she'd encountered when he had last been to the flat a couple of years earlier.

His eyes dropped to her stomach when she opened the front door. 'Lauren. Good to see you.'

'Thanks for coming over.'

'What happened?'

She led the way into the living room. 'I was watching TV, and the next thing...' She waved casually at the window as though it was a normal occurrence, before taking the brick from the sideboard.

His eyes widened. 'Were you hurt?'

She shook her head. She knew she might so easily have been; the living room wasn't exactly big, and the sofa was just to the side of the window. Had her furniture been arranged differently, things could have been much worse. 'Bit of a shock, that's all.'

'Have you called the police?'

She had prepared herself for this question, knowing that it would arise at some point, as it had with the neighbour. 'Yeah,' she lied. 'Not much they can do about it, I don't suppose.'

Karim exhaled noisily and ran a hand across his head, shedding a fine cloud of dust from his hair. 'Probably kids messing about.'

'Probably. I heard a few drunk people passing not long before it happened.'

'Seems strange for this street, though. It's always been quiet round here.' His eyes moved inadvertently once again to her stomach. 'I didn't realise you were expecting, by the way. Congratulations.'

'Thank you.'

'When's it due?'

'Twenty-second of May.'

'Boy or girl?'

'Don't know. Keeping it a surprise.'

He smiled through his obvious awkwardness, neither of them knowing what to say next. 'Look,' he said, eventually breaking the silence, 'I know someone who can get the window sorted, hopefully today. I'll give him a call.'

He reached into his pocket for his mobile phone before heading to the kitchen, leaving Lauren alone in the living room. When he returned, he told her someone would be there before 6 p.m. 'He's a mate of mine, but he's out on a job and won't be able to make it until then. Are you going to be okay?'

Lauren nodded.

'And I've sorted out payment with him already, so you don't need to worry about that.'

'It's fine. I don't want charity. I just thought it right to let you know, that's all.'

'It isn't charity. It's my property, so it's my problem.'

The urge to object further was thwarted by thoughts of her anaemic bank account. It was embarrassing to even think that she was grateful for the help. 'Thank you.'

He headed for the living room door. 'If you need anything else, just give me a call, okay?'

After Karim had left, Lauren went back to the living room.

She was safe here. No one knew where she was. These two things were the foundations upon which her life here had been built, and now neither of them was true.

You can't run for ever.

The words echoed around the room, threatening to deafen her. Whoever had put that brick through the window, it meant only one thing. She'd been found.

SIX

THE MIDWIFE

Jackie had gone home to bed after her shift had ended, but she hadn't been able to get much rest. The people in the flat next door to hers had a dog that was left alone all day while they were at work, and its relentless barking meant sleep was near impossible. There had been times she'd wondered whether her restlessness would drive her to the edge of her sanity, though she knew it wasn't only the dog that was to blame for that.

There had been chores that needed completing: washing to be taken out and hung up; food shopping to be done, though no matter how busy she kept herself, her mind insisted on making a return to the same person. Taking Lauren Coleman's number from her records on the hospital database was against protocol, but as long as no one at the unit found out about it, she'd be okay. All she needed was to keep Lauren onside, have her trust her enough to confide in her, and if she managed to get as close as she hoped, Lauren might never think to ask how she had come to get her phone number.

A couple of times during the afternoon she thought about making the call, each time finding an excuse to delay it. By early evening, she had become sick of being stuck in the flat, so she went for a drive to attempt to clear her head. Try as she might to escape her own brain, her efforts were for nothing: it was impossible. She pulled over and reached for her phone, finding the number she had stored. It was answered after just a few rings.

'Hello, is that Lauren Coleman?'

'Yes.'

'Oh, hi. It's Jackie Franklin, I'm a midwife. We met at the prenatal session you attended at the hospital.'

'Oh, hi. How are you?'

'I'm good. More importantly, how are *you*? Everything okay?'

'Fine, thanks.'

Lauren was a closed book, Jackie thought. She obviously didn't like to give too much away. It was understandable under the circumstances, and nothing Jackie hadn't been expecting.

'Look, I hope you don't mind me calling, but I just wanted to let you know about one of the groups I'm running for the mums-to-be. It's more of a social thing really, just an informal meet-up, a chance for women to get together and have a chat or discuss anything that might be concerning them. It's running weekly at High Barnet community centre. Do you think it's something you might be interested in?'

'Um... yeah.' Uncertainty stayed on the line between them, audible amid the silence. Lauren was cautious of everything, as life had taught her to be. 'Hang on, let me just find a pen and a bit of paper.'

She was unsure, Jackie thought. From what she knew of the woman, she lived a quiet life. Kept herself to herself. Sitting with a group of people and discussing her problems didn't really seem the type of thing likely to appeal to her, although Jackie knew from personal experience that there was only so long a person could endure isolation from others. Pregnancy might have changed Lauren, or maybe time itself would prove capable of that.

'How much are the sessions?' Lauren asked, returning her attention to the call.

'Nothing, there's no charge.'

She was worried about money, Jackie thought. There were also other, bigger things she was worrying about, if the leaflet that had stolen her attention at the hospital was anything to go by.

'We meet on Tuesdays,' she said, 'if you're available then.'

Tuesday was Lauren's day off, or the day she worked from home, at least. Despite her efforts to live as anonymously as possible, it had been easy enough for Jackie to find out her work pattern.

'Okay,' Lauren said non-committally. 'I'll try to make it.'

'Great. It's only a small group, just four or five of us usually. We might see you there then.'

Jackie said goodbye and hung up. She felt strangely calm, considering. The thought unsettled her. Perhaps lying was something she was inherently skilled at, and maybe that should have disconcerted her more than it did. Despite Lauren's non-committal response to the invitation to the group, Jackie felt certain that she would see her there. It would be one step closer to putting the plan in motion.

She sat back and pushed her skull against the headrest, trying to force out the pressure that had built behind her temples. Her fingers gripped the steering wheel as though the car was still in motion, and when she glanced at her whitened knuckles, it occurred to her for the first time just how much those hands were capable of. They had brought new life into the world. They had nurtured and soothed, working as a separate entity, afforded a life of their own. Her hands had served as a reflection of everything she was, carrying out their work in the way she wanted the world to see her. And yet they were also capable of betrayal.

In her lap, her phone began to ring. She glanced down at

the caller ID, then let it ring out as she turned her attention to the other side of the street, to the row of houses basking in the soft light of table lamps and television screens, the day having drawn into the cosiness of evening.

Her attention rested on number 78, on the downstairs window, where the room was partially obscured by half-closed curtains. There was a light on, and she watched as movement beyond the curtains caught her attention, a passing figure casting a shadow.

She had been there when the van had pulled up outside, and when the driver had gone in to replace the window. She had watched him at work as he'd removed the fractured panel of glass, and she had seen Lauren when she'd appeared to speak with him. The new pane had gone in, the house a safe haven once more. For now, at least.

SEVEN

THE MOTHER

Lauren looked at the time at the bottom of her computer screen. It was 3.20 p.m. and she couldn't wait to finish work for the day. The baby was unsettled this afternoon, turning and twisting, unable to get comfortable. You and me both, kid, she thought as she made herself a final decaf tea of the day.

She made a coffee for her boss and took it through to her office.

'You read my mind.' Fiona looked up through a dark mass of thick fringe. A pile of paperwork sat on the desk in front of her.

'Still working on the deal with Selfridges?' Lauren asked as she placed the coffee on the desk.

Fiona rolled her eyes. 'The never-ending contract negotiation. These people drive a hard bargain.'

Her eyes narrowed as she scrutinised Lauren's appearance. Lauren knew that in her oversized cardigan and maternity leggings she was hardly the representation of her fashion brand Fiona would choose. During the previous eighteen months, the online company had begun its move into high street department stores, but Selfridges was the gold ticket she'd been working years towards.

'You look tired.'

Thanks, Lauren thought. She might have softened the indirect insult somehow, but that had never really been Fiona's way of going about things.

'Comes with pregnancy, apparently.'

'Are you feeling okay?'

'I'm fine,' she lied. She could hardly tell her about the brick through the window, so sticking with the subject of the pregnancy seemed the safest option.

'How many weeks left until your leave?'

'Seven.' Not that she was counting them down or anything, she thought. She planned to work until a fortnight before her due date, which would allow her to have more time off after the baby was born. Her salary might be meagre, but she was grateful to have a job that was steady and secure, something she knew was rare to find.

'If you need to go off any earlier, just let me know, okay?'

'Thanks. It should be fine, though.'

'Could you reschedule my appointment with the web designer tomorrow afternoon?' Fiona gestured to the paperwork in front of her. 'This needs all my attention.'

'Will do.'

The Tube from Covent Garden was even busier than usual, commuters squeezed in next to one another and the hot air filled with the stench of fried onions. The smell made Lauren's stomach turn. A swell of people departed the carriage when they reached Finsbury Park. As she was stepping onto the platform, Lauren felt a shove in the small of her back. It knocked her off balance and sent her crashing into the commuter in front of her, whose reaction was less than charitable.

'For fuck's sake.' He turned sharply, his bag swinging from his shoulder. He looked ready to say something else before he registered the pregnant stomach and retracted the response, opting instead for an impatient sigh.

Lauren eyed a teenage boy weaving his way aggressively through the crowd of people, presumably the person who'd just shoved her. She was hit by the familiarity of him, her stomach twisting in a knot at how similar he looked from behind to her brother, or at least how Jamie had looked as a boy. The knot undid itself, replaced by a rush of relief at the thought that it hadn't been a targeted attack; she had just been in the way.

'I'm fine, by the way,' she sniped at the man who'd just sworn at her. 'Thanks for asking, though.'

She pushed her bag up on her shoulder and made her way to the station exit, desperate to be out in the fresh air. This was one of the downsides of life in London, she thought, the impatience of everyone, the rush to be somewhere and be doing something. No one cared too much for those around them, and what had once attracted her about the place often now repelled her.

Out on the street, she paused outside a coffee shop to catch her breath.

As a woman left the shop, its warming aroma drifted out onto the street behind her. Lauren gave in to its appeal and went inside to order herself something, knowing she needed to be mindful now of every penny. She asked for a decaf cappuccino, and while she was waiting for the barista to prepare it, her phone rang in her handbag. It was a withheld number. She answered. There was silence for a moment, then she heard someone breathing at the other end of the line.

'Hello,' she said for a second time. 'Who is this?'

As before, there was no response. A moment later, the call was ended. Lauren returned her phone to her bag and looked around her. She was being paranoid, she thought, but then the last few days had given her good reason.

She went to a seat in the corner, in no rush to go home to

her empty flat. Thoughts of Jamie consumed her. It had been a long time since she'd contacted him, their relationship consigned firmly to the past. Despite what he'd done, she still sometimes wondered about him. Was it ever too late for someone to turn their life around? For Jamie, she feared the answer was yes.

She had known for the last few years where he was working. He had been assigned a probation officer after his release from prison, and she had spoken with the man a few times, keen to know how her brother was getting on, though far less keen to see him. Jamie had lived in the same bedsit since leaving prison. As far as she knew, he was still there. Lauren had never visited him while he'd been inside, and she hadn't seen him since his release. For a long time she had lived too far away to make the journey, but now within travelling distance, she couldn't bring herself to make contact. What would she say to him? Where would they even start?

But if she never tried, she would never know. She ran an internet search for the pizza restaurant in Milton Keynes. She called the number without allowing herself a chance to deliberate over the decision. It was answered after just a couple of rings.

'Is it possible to speak to Jamie?'

'Hang on. I'll give him a shout.'

She felt her heart begin to race. She hadn't expected him to be there. He had the night off; it was the wrong restaurant. Whatever she'd assumed before making the call, the last thing she'd expected to happen was to actually hear his voice.

She couldn't go through with it. As she ended the call, she felt sick at the thought that nagged at her, taunting her with its repeated threat. He blamed her for what happened to him. If he hadn't gone to prison that first time, his life might have been so different. And if it hadn't been for her, he would never have been inside. She was responsible... was that still how he saw things? So what if he now knew where she was? He might know about the baby; he might begrudge her the happiness the future now promised her. What if Jamie was the person who'd put that brick through her window?

By the time Lauren got home, she'd exhausted herself with thoughts of Jamie's potential desire for revenge. When she reached the flat, there was a box on the front door. It was wrapped in brown paper and addressed to her. She took it into the flat and ripped off the paper. Inside was a box from a designer baby clothing company, the kind of place Lauren had idly browsed online, knowing she could never afford so much as a packet of socks from there. Even the box was beautiful: white and shiny and tied with a gold satin ribbon.

She undid the ribbon and took off the lid, the breath leaving her as she saw what waited inside. A gift set, all in grey: Baby-gro, booties and bib. All shredded to pieces. All covered in blood.

EIGHT

THE MIDWIFE

The woman's screams were raw and visceral. It had been too late to give her an epidural – by the time she'd come into the hospital, labour had already been well established, with contractions coming every ninety seconds – and though staff were limited with the painkiller options they were able to offer, she had kept demanding more, the mantra of her yelled and desperate pleas a mechanism to try to cope with the pain.

Sandra was on the shift with Jackie again that evening, two of their younger colleagues dealing with another delivery at the other end of the corridor. Whatever she had wanted to ask Jackie at the end of their last shift together, she seemed to have forgotten about it now. It couldn't have been important – certainly not any of the things that Jackie had feared. If Sandra had any suspicions about her move to the hospital, they had for now at least been pushed to one side.

Sandra had moved between the two delivery rooms at first, leaving Jackie with one expectant mother while she went to check on the progress of the other. Now, with the woman having been fully dilated for a couple of hours already, she was checking the baby's heart rate as Jackie tried to calm the increasingly fractious mother.

'You've done this all before,' she said, taking the woman's hand and squeezing it gently. 'You can do it again. You're doing it.'

Opposite her, on the other side of the bed, the husband's face had turned pale. He looked almost as much in need of medical assistance as his wife, the dark circles beneath his eyes a telltale sign of fatigue and weariness. The couple already had toddler twins; the sleep deprivation that would come with having a newborn would be nothing they weren't apparently already accustomed to. The twins had been delivered via a Caesarean section that had taken the mother months to recover from, and with three children soon to care for, she had been adamant that this baby would be delivered naturally. Watching as she buckled in agony, Jackie wondered whether the right decision had been made.

Until a few minutes earlier, the man had been repeatedly telling his wife to keep breathing; now, having been sharply reprimanded for his clichéd efforts, he had fallen silent, momentarily redundant.

Jackie reached for the gas and air and handed it to the woman, who grabbed the mouthpiece from her as though she might use it to hit someone. Sandra looked up from the bottom of the bed and gave Jackie a look she recognised all too well, one no midwife ever wanted to see. The baby was in distress. Time was against them.

The husband caught the look. 'What?' he said, appealing to Jackie. 'What's wrong?'

She raised a hand to calm him – the last thing they needed was for him to panic his wife – then turned back to the woman. 'You really need to push. You've got to give this everything now, okay? Hold my hand again.'

On the other side of the bed, the husband took her other

hand. Jackie felt the woman's nails embed themselves in her palm. She pushed a thick clump of matted hair from her damp forehead as she encouraged her with gentle words, her voice a note of calm in the fraught atmosphere. It took an effort to free her hand from the mother's grip so that she could go to Sandra's aid, but when she did, she saw the crown of the baby's head. They needed to get him out.

Another scream and she returned to the mother's side. 'All that energy you're using on those screams, we need them to push this baby out. He's desperate to meet you, Mum.'

As she took the woman's hand again, she felt the force of the pressure as though passed from one body to another. The woman shuddered with the effort and another scream ripped from her. Two more followed as the baby's head finally pushed free from her body. There was a moment of awful silence that seemed to last too long. Then a cry. A single, sharp newborn wail that cut through the room.

Sandra held the little boy and gestured to his father. 'Dad, are you going to cut the cord?'

The mother wouldn't remember this, Jackie thought. These next few minutes would be a blur of relief and exhaustion; there would be nothing between the pain and the first cuddle with her child, those precious moments of skin-to-skin contact when the rest of the world would cease to exist. She had been witness to it countless times over the years, always conscious of her position as an outsider; an intruder on an intimacy that was exclusive to the delivery room.

Sandra passed Jackie the baby as she attended to the mother. Jackie held the new life in her hands as she had done on so many occasions, the enormity of the moment often lost to the rush and urgency of the delivery room. Skinny bloodstained limbs rested against her arms as she stared at the tiny boy. Limbs like branches, she thought. How strong they might grow, given the chance. How much possibility this child might have ahead of him.

'Jackie?'

Sandra's voice woke her from her reverie. The child's father was watching her, and when she looked to his wife, her face was pale and drawn, her eyes narrowed with a mistrust Jackie wasn't accustomed to receiving. She forced a smile and carried the baby to his mother, placing him in her arms. She watched the rush of love that swelled between the two of them, the brief moment of awkwardness dispelled instantaneously. Tears ran down the woman's face, the pain of the delivery already consigned to the past. Jackie averted her eyes and went to the sink, where she scrubbed her hands with soapy water that was too hot. She watched her fingers turn red, numb to the scorching of her skin. She closed her eyes, and for a moment she felt nothing.

After the baby had been fed, cleaned and weighed, and the mother had been stitched and given something to eat, Jackie went to the toilets and locked herself inside a cubicle. She leaned against the door and took a deep breath. Her head pounded with tension that had been building behind her temples all evening, and she felt sick with an anxiety that refused to be shaken. Her hand was bruised, a patch of grey skin circling her palm. When she closed her eyes, snapshots of a nightmare returned to her: bed sheets, pain, blood so red it shone through the darkness.

She used the toilet. There was blood on her sleeve that had gone unnoticed when she'd washed her hands in the delivery room. She scrubbed it at the sink, smearing the red to a watery pink, the stain refusing to shift as the last of the colour washed away down the plughole.

The door opened: one of the younger midwives, a woman Jackie was not yet familiar with. She smiled, but it faded quickly as she took in Jackie's appearance: the dishevelled hair, the pale complexion, the reddened eyes that betrayed her tiredness.

'Everything okay?' she asked, as Jackie quickly rearranged her hair.

'Fine.'

'Sandra said you did a great job in there. Whatever you said to the mother, you managed to calm her down.'

'I didn't do anything really.'

The young woman smiled again, but Jackie sensed there was something else behind it. Suspicion. She felt her face flush with her own guilt.

The other midwife went into one of the cubicles, and Jackie splashed her face with cold water. Appear one thing while being another, she reminded herself. She could do this. She was already doing it.

NINE

THE MOTHER

On Tuesday, Lauren attended the group Jackie had invited her to. There had been nothing in the arrangement to work remotely on Tuesdays that specified this meant at home, so she'd made sure to get ahead of herself that morning, responding to emails and making appointments. Now she checked the volume on her phone was loud enough that she would hear it, should anyone call her.

She knew why she'd been invited to the group. Jackie had sensed her anxiety at the hospital the day they'd met. While everyone else had worn smiles of excitement and anticipation, Lauren had felt the fear in her own face, and it must have been visible, to Jackie at least. Now, with the brick through her window and the box of bloodied baby clothes left at her door, Lauren feared it would be visible to everyone.

When Lauren arrived, Jackie was there with another woman, who she introduced as Amber. She was younger than Lauren, early to mid thirties, her frame small and slender, her bump pronounced alongside her thin limbs. She had a mass of shoulder-length curly hair that was highlighted with pink streaks, and she wore the denim dungarees that Lauren noticed seemed to be a staple garment for pregnant women. They made small talk for a while as they waited for the others, but ten minutes after the start of the session time, Jackie went to her bag to check her phone.

'Louise's son has been sick, so she can't make it,' she explained when she returned.

'And Hannah?' Amber asked.

Jackie shrugged. 'Not heard anything from her.'

'Do you know the other women then?' Lauren asked, hoping she wouldn't find herself playing gooseberry in an established friendship group.

'Only Hannah,' Amber told her. 'In passing, you know. We don't really know each other that well.'

'We may as well make a start then,' Jackie said with a smile. 'I'm Jackie, as you both already know. I've been a midwife for over twenty years now, but I also run baby groups and antenatal classes. I know this can be an incredibly anxious time for pregnant women, but it still seems there's not enough opportunity for people to talk about their concerns. I don't know why that is, although having spoken to so many mums-to-be over the years, the feedback seems to be that there's an expectation of positivity and cheeriness, as though talking about fears or worries might make a woman seem ungrateful or undeserving in some way.'

Lauren glanced sideways at Amber, who was nodding her head. 'Yep. I mean, I'm supposed to feel all glowing, aren't I, but look at me.'

'How's the nausea now?' Jackie asked.

'Still waiting for it to leave. I've resigned myself to the fact that it's not going to, not until the baby's here, anyway.'

'You look really well,' Lauren told her. 'I know that can't mean much if you're not feeling great.'

'Face full of make-up. Hides a million sins. How's your pregnancy been? Any sickness?'

'Other than the constant tiredness, I've felt pretty good,'

Lauren said, feeling guilty now for admitting it. There had been a couple of days of nausea early on, before the ten-week mark, but thankfully she had managed to avoid any sickness. 'I've been lucky.'

'Everyone's luck runs dry eventually,' Amber said. She smiled at Lauren, though the look managed to be somehow vacant. 'Anyway, don't mention the tiredness to anyone – they'll just remind you that it gets worse once the baby arrives. Same as birthing stories, have you noticed that? Why is it that when you're pregnant, everyone wants to tell you their horror stories? I don't really want to hear about labours on the side of motorways or blood-filled baths, thanks all the same. Give me your stories of eight-minute pain-free deliveries, please.'

Lauren saw Jackie watching Amber, her eyes seemingly fixed on the other woman's lips as her words spilled from her. Was Amber scared of the prospect of labour? Weren't all first-time mothers? But Lauren didn't know whether Amber was already a mother. She might have been through all this before.

'Is this your first child?' she asked.

Amber nodded. 'Might be the last, too. I didn't sign up for all this sickness.' She smiled again. 'Pay me no attention. I deal with everything with humour. You'd go mad otherwise, wouldn't you? And what about you? Is it your first baby, I mean, not are you mad?'

Lauren nodded. 'And yes to the madness too, maybe.'

'Are you worried about the birth, Amber?' Jackie asked.

'Terrified. I mean, that's what everyone's answer should be if they're honest, right? It's all the things that could go wrong.'

'Things do occasionally go wrong,' Jackie admitted. 'But there's a tiny chance of that happening. With most deliveries, mother and baby are fine. And that'll be the case here too, I'm sure.'

Lauren felt Jackie's eyes on her as she spoke, though she found herself unable to return the contact. The midwife had seen that leaflet in her hand; she knew Lauren was concerned about the things that might happen. Why was this woman she barely knew so keen to offer her reassurance?

'I know this will sound clichéd,' Jackie added, 'but stress is counterproductive and can make things worse than they need to be. I always recommend that pregnant women take some time out for themselves at least once a week if they can. Do something that will promote relaxation and destressing. Yoga is a good one – there are plenty of antenatal yoga classes about. Swimming is always beneficial too. Have either of you ever tried meditation?'

Amber shook her head. She didn't seem to Lauren the type to meditate, though she wasn't really sure what that 'type' was.

'You can try any of these from home,' Jackie said. 'Except the swimming, obviously. But I do recommend trying to get out and join a class instead. It's always good to be around other people.'

'If they turn up,' Amber said with a laugh.

The atmosphere seemed to chill with the comment, Jackie's lip curling as she checked her phone to look at the time.

'Time for a tea break?' Jackie suggested, looking up from her phone. 'I've got decaf.'

She got up to go to the table, and Amber and Lauren followed. Jackie poured the tea and offered them biscuits, putting a hand on Lauren's arm as she reached past her for a spare plate.

'Your baby's going to be fine,' she said, her words almost a whisper in Lauren's ear. 'I promise you.'

Lauren smiled and took the drink Jackie offered her before returning to her seat. She tried to pull her mind from the bloodied clothes that had been left on her doorstep. She had disposed of them in a bin at the back of a restaurant off the high street. She didn't want to think about where the blood might have come from.

'Have you watched that series that's just been on?' Amber said. 'I can't remember the title, but it's got that woman in it, you know, the blonde one who seems to be in everything.'

'She's a great actress,' Jackie said. 'I know the one you mean, though I can't remember her name either.'

Lauren sat silently as the other two women discussed the programme. Her thoughts were random and disconnected: the baby, the brick, the clothing, Jamie. Wherever her mind took her, her thoughts returned to him, some invisible pull drawing her back to the possibility that he may have made a silent return to her life.

When she tuned back into the conversation, Amber was talking to Jackie about her mother.

'I remember her telling me about my brother's birth. Gave me nightmares for months, though I'm sure it wasn't as bad as she made out. She probably used it as a scare story to keep me away from boys.'

Though it was Amber speaking, Lauren's focus rested on Jackie. She wondered what it was about the woman that invited trust. There was something reassuring about her nature – something maternal that exuded warmth.

'Anyway,' Amber concluded, 'not sure how we ended up there. What about you, Lauren? Your mother share her birthing nightmares with you?'

Lauren forced a thin smile. 'Thankfully not.' She wasn't going to tell them that her mother was dead. Her single-parent status already gained her sympathy she didn't want or need.

Amber reached into her pocket and checked her phone for the time. 'I'd better go. Don't want to miss my bus. It was lovely to meet you, Lauren.'

'And you. See you next week.'

'Thank you for inviting me today,' Lauren said to Jackie once the two of them were alone. 'It's been good just to chat.'

'Are you feeling any better about things?'

She nodded, although it wasn't entirely true. No amount of talking could alleviate the fears she held buried in her chest.

'Sometimes it's easier to talk to strangers too, isn't it? Look, you've got my number if you need anything.'

'Thank you.'

'Same time next week?'

'Great. See you then.'

Lauren was nearing the Tube station when her phone began ringing. She stopped and stepped aside to let people pass, her heart quickening at the sight of the words 'withheld number'.

She answered hurriedly, her fingers fumbling across the lit screen. 'Who the hell is this?' she hissed. Her body braced for the sound of Jamie's voice, though she knew he was unlikely to speak.

'Lauren?'

Her heart dropped like a stone. *You idiot*, she chided herself. 'Karim? I'm so sorry. I thought...' She allowed her sentence to trail away, unsure how she was going to justify her response.

'I was just calling to see if you're okay after what happened.'

He sounded affronted, and Lauren didn't blame him. It was hardly the reception he would have been expecting.

'I'm fine,' she said. 'Thanks for checking in. I'm sorry, I just...' Again she didn't know what to say. She couldn't tell him that someone kept phoning her and not saying anything, in the same way she couldn't tell him about that note around the brick.

'The window's been okay since it went in?' he asked, diverting attention from her awkwardness.

'Yes, there's been no problems.'

'Okay. Great.' There was a pause, in which she sensed he wanted to say something more. 'You know where I am if you need anything,' he eventually added.

'I appreciate that. Thank you.'

When he ended the call, Lauren returned her phone to her bag, wondering why she felt so annoyed with herself and why she was disappointed with the way Karim had signed off from the conversation. She'd been hoping for something more, though the attraction she felt towards him felt misplaced and ill-timed.

She got back to the cold and silent flat. Her hand roamed to her stomach, her palm resting on the curve of her baby's back. She already loved her child more than she had ever loved anyone else, and yet the thought that her pregnancy was an act of selfishness struck her with a force that threatened to knock her over. It took a village to raise a child, wasn't that how the saying went? Who else would her child have? The idea that she would be all it needed was an unrealistic notion, driven by a need that was hers alone. She had romanticised their future together, picturing the kind of scenes played out in Hallmark films. The reality of parenting was entirely different, and what would her child think of her in fifteen years' time if he or she found out the lie it had been unwittingly involved in? She was bringing a new life into the charade of her own existence, wilfully inflicting all its fakery on an unsuspecting and innocent child who might in some way reap the consequences of everything she was responsible for.

She didn't deserve this baby, but it was too late to think like that now.

TEN

THE MIDWIFE

Jackie lay in a puddle of blood that hadn't yet woken her. Her hand rested lightly at the barely-there curve of her stomach, a protective palm placed near her unborn child. A child she would never get to meet. She observed herself as though floating above her own body, her dream transporting her to the memory of the place. This had happened to her before, this kind of half dream, half-lived experience, and no matter how hard she tried to fight against the vision, she knew she would be unable to escape it, and that it would remain with her until it was ready to let her go. She watched herself stir from sleep, saw herself open her eyes and register the feeling of wetness between her legs; the dark stain that spread across the sheet beneath her. The scream woke her before she realised that it didn't come from the dream, it was alive and real in the room with her. It *was* her.

She pushed herself up in the bed and brought her knees to her chest, heart pounding and ears still ringing as she tried to catch her breath. Disorientated, she sought the details of the room amid the darkness, realising with each silhouette of every familiar item of furniture that she wasn't where she had thought she was. Her reality crashed upon her, those past decades emptying themselves with a crushing weight that always threatened to suffocate her with its finality. She was in the flat in Oakwood in London, alone. This wasn't the house in which she had spent all those years; there was no one beside her on the other side of the bed. Simon was gone, their life together evaporated; all the dreams and hopes that had filled their home cleared out with the furniture and the recriminations.

She got out of bed and went to the bathroom, where she splashed her face with cold water. When she went through to the kitchen and looked at the clock on the windowsill, she realised it was later than she had thought, though it was still only 4.30 a.m. Her shift started in a few hours' time, but she knew she couldn't stay in the flat between now and then; the silence and solitude of the place would drive her insane.

She showered quickly and threw on a pair of jeans and an oversized jumper before packing her uniform into a bag. The street was deserted and still dark, sunrise having yet to push over the roofs of the terraces. She drove with the radio off, the voice of the overenthusiastic presenter who greeted her when the engine went on too cheerful and misplaced for the time of morning.

When she got to the hospital, the ward was eerily quiet. One of her colleagues was sitting at a computer, its bright screen illuminating the otherwise dimly lit corner of the neonatal unit's reception area. She nodded a greeting and glanced at the time on the screen as Jackie approached. 'Couldn't sleep?'

'Something like that.' Jackie shrugged off her coat. 'The early bird and all that.'

'Urgh. I can't wait to finish.'

'Busy night?'

Her colleague shook her head. 'Too quiet. They always seem longer then, don't they?'

Jackie smiled but said nothing. She knew only too well how

long and drawn out the quiet nights could be; she had been living with them for long enough.

A door along the corridor opened, and one of the other midwives appeared. Jackie waved a silent greeting before going and putting her things in a locker. She made herself a strong cup of black coffee in the kitchen and took it through to the staff room. There was no one there, which was exactly how she had hoped to find it. She closed the door behind her and moved the mouse beside the keyboard, waiting for the screen to come to life. After typing in her login details, she accessed the patient database.

The online system was much the same as it had been in the last hospital where she'd worked, though there were differences she would need to familiarise herself with. As the rest of the unit started to wake and the first sounds of morning began to infiltrate the silence, she searched for the name Lauren Coleman again, bringing up the files relating to the expectant mother: appointment history, scan results, personal details.

At the sound of someone at the office door, she minimised the screen.

'Morning.' One of her colleagues breezed in as though it wasn't still the early hours, her energy something Jackie wished was contagious. She glanced around her, searching for a security camera she might have missed. It seemed too coincidental that every time she tried to access Lauren's details, another staff member appeared to interrupt her. She watched as the woman started to rummage about in the filing cabinet. 'Haven't seen any Sellotape anywhere, have you?'

'Tried the kitchen?' Jackie suggested. 'I think there might be some on top of the microwave.'

The woman rolled her eyes and smiled. 'Of course. Where everyone keeps it. Thanks.'

Jackie waited for her to leave before returning her attention to the computer screen. What did her colleagues make of her so far? she wondered. Quiet, unassuming, conscientious. Well-intentioned.

She thought of the innocent little life that was growing inside Lauren's womb, blissfully ignorant of what awaited it. Her attention returned to the computer screen, where her eyes rested on the name in front of her.

Lauren Coleman. 41 years old. Unmarried. Currently employed as a PA.

A pretty name – average and unassuming. Nothing unusual that might draw attention. She studied it as though it might somehow offer her answers, then glanced at the clock; her shift wasn't due to start for over half an hour.

A poster on the far wall caught her eye. *Becoming a parent*, its heading read. It showed a woman cradling a newborn, her arm curved protectively around her sleeping child. A man stood beside her, his hand on her shoulder. Key words jumped out at Jackie. *Unconditional... empowering... happiness.* In her lap, her fingers curled into a fist. She grimaced as she fought back a wave of hot, angry tears, then swiped a hand across the desk, sending paperwork and stationery flying; a mug someone had left there smashing to the floor.

Lauren Coleman. A new home, a new life, a new name. A second chance at happiness – the kind of second chance Jackie herself had never been afforded.

ELEVEN

THE MOTHER

On Saturday, Lauren went to an out-of-town retail park to buy some clothes for the baby. It was the final thing she needed in preparation for her child's arrival, and though she'd looked at things online, distracting herself from unwanted thoughts with images of cute sleep suits and pram shoes no bigger than a doll's, buying these things from websites wasn't the same as choosing them in a shop.

She had underestimated the enormity of entering the place. She had never been to a shop like this before – she had never had any reason to – and she hesitated just beyond the automatic doors, her senses hit by a rush of colour and sound: clothing in every shade of the rainbow; bedding adorned with animals and fairies; mobiles turning stars and moons as they hummed out soothing lullabies. *Something is going to go wrong,* the voice inside her head told her. *You are not going to make it that far.*

She clenched her jaw as she forced back a wave of tears that threatened to escape her. *Stop it,* she told herself. *Stop doing this to yourself.*

As she lingered by a range of extortionately priced travel

systems, she felt grateful that she had managed to keep her spend on essential items to a minimum. Even so, babies came with a price tag, and the cost of the IVF treatment had been financially draining. When it came to the inevitable move she and her child would be facing in maybe less than a year's time, she was planning to travel as lightly as it was possible to with a small human being.

The thought made her take a step back towards the shop door. What was she doing here? Didn't she already have everything she needed? She felt a sudden rush of heat flood from her chest to her throat, aware that her face was colouring pink as she stood there. One of the shop assistants approached her, sensing her uncertainty, and when she asked whether she needed help, Lauren found herself tripping over a response, her reply barely coherent.

'Thanks anyway,' she mumbled, and hurried for the exit, relieved when she was outside and away from all the paraphernalia of parenthood that had closed around her.

As she made her way back to the bus stop, she almost walked straight into Callum. Or rather, he almost walked straight into her, barely able to see past the large box he was carrying propped against his chest.

'I'm so sorry,' he apologised hastily as he moved the box aside, still clearly not having realised that it was her. There was a picture of a barbecue on the side of the box: one of the grill types that was supposed to cook everything a little more healthily than the traditional models. Lauren wasn't sure why such an innocuous purchase bothered her, but the jab to the gut was undeniable. The domesticity of the item seemed irrationally like a personal attack.

At last recognition dawned. 'Lauren.'

She watched his sharp blue eyes dart to the window of the shop she had just left, to the nursery that was set up on display there: the white cot, the neutral grey bedding, the animal mobile. There was a flicker of something she couldn't decipher before he looked back at her, his focus moving briefly but unmissably to her stomach. Shock? Rejection? She was showing prominently now, her bump no longer hidden beneath her clothing.

'Oh my God.'

His eyes searched hers for an explanation, every conversation and argument that had come to shape their relationship now returning to haunt them both, the memories so alive that they might have been re-enacted in the car park beside them.

'You're...' He fell silent, and there was no need for her to confirm it. 'God,' he said again. 'Congratulations.'

There was no sincerity in the expression; it was merely an expected response, the right word at the right moment to fill what would otherwise have been an even more uncomfortable silence. The truth was that whatever he really wanted to say was likely to have been swallowed down with his shock.

Was it me? Was it just that you didn't want a child with me?

'Callum—'

She was interrupted by an echo, his name spoken by another woman's voice just feet behind him. A tall blonde appeared at his side, armed with an array of shopping bags. 'I thought you'd have got that back to the car by now,' she said. She looked at Lauren. 'Hi.'

Now the barbecue felt even more of an insult, as though its purchase was designed purely to hurt her. Ridiculous, she chided herself, but pain coursed through her with unprecedented fierceness. She imagined Callum and this woman sharing dinner in a beautiful mature garden, two steaks cooking on the grill beside an open bottle of wine. She would wear a summer dress that skimmed perfect tanned thighs; he would laugh at a joke she made before putting an arm around her waist and kissing her. He would consider himself so fortunate; he would muse on what a lucky escape he'd had. The image her brain had conjured was too ludicrously idyllic to be believable, like something out of a TV advertisement, but she was too hurt to find any humour in it.

'Anyway, good to see you,' Callum said hurriedly, clearly not keen on the idea of introducing his girlfriend to his ex. He turned towards his car, walking away as though she was just someone he'd met once, a distant memory from an even more distant past. Perhaps that was how he saw her now – someone from another lifetime.

Lauren watched the woman as she opened the boot of the car and stepped aside to let Callum put the box down. She was beautiful, Lauren thought. Younger than her, too. The thought smarted. Just how much younger was she? Young enough to consider a future with children? Young enough to give him the life Lauren never would have been able to?

She hurried away, suddenly aware of the fact that she had been standing there staring, and that either one of them might turn and see her doing so. By the time she got to the bus stop, she'd forgotten why she'd even gone to the shops. Whatever it was no longer seemed important. She and the baby could manage without it; as long as they had each other, everything was going to be okay.

On the bus, a teenage couple sat a few seats ahead of her, heads tilted towards one another as they listened to a shared set of headphones. The girl turned to say something to the boy, who smiled before kissing her gently on the cheek. Lauren felt her face burn. There was something so innocent about them, something not yet ruined by the cynicism of the world. Her thoughts strayed to Karim, wondering whether he was with anyone. The thought caught her off guard. He was nothing to do with her. Why would she care whether he was in a relationship? She reached into her bag for her phone and found his number.

I'm sorry about the other day, she tapped. *Your number came up as withheld. I've been getting nuisance calls, but I shouldn't have answered like that. Hope all is okay with you.*

She pressed send without thinking about it or allowing herself time to change her mind. 'Nuisance calls' covered a whole host of possibilities, hopefully sufficient to explain her reaction without offering a hint that the calls she'd received weren't random. Perhaps she wouldn't get a reply. There'd been no part of her text that had required one.

She looked up again at the young couple, and when the boy turned his head to say something to his girlfriend, he caught her staring. She looked away, embarrassed, and when the bus reached her stop, she avoided looking at them as she passed. She hurried home, trying to free herself from thoughts of Callum. She had loved him more than she had ever loved any man. She had still loved him when she'd left him, and that was why she'd had to say goodbye.

Karim texted back when she was nearly at the flat. *Don't worry, all forgotten,* he'd written. *I hate those calls!* The exclamation mark seemed a little overenthusiastic, or perhaps she was just reading too much into it.

When she opened her front door, an envelope was waiting on the hallway floor. There was no name on it, no address, and when she slipped the single A4 sheet of paper from inside it, she found a printout of a newspaper article, the headline of which made her heart stop in her chest.

TEENAGER BEATEN AND LEFT TO DIE

She steadied herself with a hand against the wall, gulping air into her lungs as she tried to catch her breath. The rest of the article swam in front of her, the text merging into a blur of print. She scrunched the sheet in her hand and closed her fist around it, crushing it until it became invisible. If only she could make it go away with such little effort.

Her palm was hot and sweating, the paper sparking a heat that inflamed her skin. The words screamed at her, taunting, but she wouldn't read any more. She didn't need to. She already knew exactly what had happened.

TWELVE

THE MIDWIFE

They never met at either of their homes, keeping their territory neutral by going to hotels. Besides, Peter still lived in Hampshire, too long a journey to make meeting near his home a possibility. It had felt seedy to begin with – it still did, because that was what it was, she supposed, their relationship constricted to covert conversations and secret liaisons, played out with all the underhand secrecy of an office affair. Had the circumstances been different, she imagined some people might have found it exciting, but Jackie had never been a thrill-seeker, and this was something that could cost her everything.

That day, they met in a small B and B on the outskirts of Whetstone, checking in separately to different rooms. Jackie paid for her own, despite Peter's insistence that it was only fair he foot the bill. Though she wouldn't actually use the room, she didn't want to feel indebted to him in any way, and having his name and card details linked to her booking would only have drawn attention to them if anything was to go wrong.

She sat on the side of the bed and nursed a takeaway cup of coffee, the hotel room's offering so poor that Peter had gone out to find a café.

'How does she seem?' he asked as he sat beside her.

'Fine. I mean, to speak to her, you'd never think anything was amiss. I suppose that's the most frightening part.'

Peter traced his fingertips along her bare shoulder. 'She still trusts you?'

'I've no reason to think otherwise.'

'You've got to keep her onside, Jac. If she starts to suspect anything—'

'She won't,' she interrupted, a little too abruptly. 'I promise you. She trusts me.'

He leaned towards the bedside table and put his drink down. 'For how long, that's the question. She's volatile.'

Jackie turned to him. He seemed older than he had done just a couple of weeks ago. This woman was getting to him more than he would admit. So many years had passed, yet he couldn't let her go. 'I'm worried about you,' she admitted. 'She's become an obsession.'

'What do you think I should do then? Just let her go? We both know where that led last time.'

She got up and put her coffee beside his. 'You're certain she's responsible?' she asked, though there was little need for the question. How many times had he told her that he had never been surer of anything else in his life? 'Everything you've told me... there's no mistake?'

'How many mistakes have you ever known me to make?'

From anyone else, the statement might have sounded arrogant, but for Peter it was true, and he had earned the right to claim it. The problem was that too many people were yet to realise that fact.

'Show me again.'

Jackie had seen the documents before, so many times that she was able to recall entire sections. Despite this, Peter responded to her request. He got up and retrieved his bag from the chair in the corner. Unzipping it, he pulled out an A4-sized folder that he brought back to the bed with him. Jackie sat beside him and waited as he riffled through its pages, stopping at one she was already familiar with. It was an article from a local newspaper in Brighton, dated thirteen years earlier.

Young Woman Drowned at Home, the headline read. *A 23-year-old-woman was found dead at her home in the early hours of Sunday morning, following a party at the property. Emergency services were called to the house when one of the woman's housemates found her unconscious in the bath. Police are investigating the circumstances of the death.*

Jackie knew the details of the reports that followed. The woman was later named as Becky Hargreaves, and the post-mortem investigation revealed high levels of alcohol and Ecstasy in her bloodstream. The party had been a wild one; things had got out of control. Becky's devastated friends and housemates had given mixed statements about the events of the night, all of which reflected the fact that everyone present had been too intoxicated to offer an accurate account of what had happened.

As Jackie flipped from one report to the next, scanning once again the details of the case, she felt Peter's focus resting on the side of her face. 'Becky Hargreaves' death was no accident,' he said. 'I know it, and there are others who know it. Someone else who was there that night must be aware of what happened. There's one person who knows the truth, at least.'

She closed the file and placed it on the bed beside her. 'And you don't think Becky was the only one?'

He shook his head solemnly. 'I know she wasn't. Daniel Thorne. An ex-boyfriend. Seems an awful coincidence, doesn't it? Unless she's so unlucky that death has a habit of following her around. My gut has never been wrong, Jac – you know that. If I had even the slightest shred of doubt, I wouldn't have contacted you. And you know I would never ask all this of you if I thought there was another way.'

He put his hands on her shoulders, and their eyes met. 'She's a killer, Jac. She's done it before. She'll do it again.'

THIRTEEN

THE MOTHER

That evening, when Lauren went to make herself a cup of tea, she found that the little milk that remained in the fridge door had gone off, its curdled stench making her stomach churn in protest. It was a stupid, inconsequential matter, but in that moment, running out of fresh milk seemed disproportionately important, and she felt a wave of frustration that she realised wasn't caused by the milk alone. Perhaps it was fate's way of telling her she didn't need tea at this time of evening, though she'd been drinking decaf long before finding out she was pregnant. Either way, she wanted a cup, so she found her jacket and her keys and left the flat.

There was a car parked on the opposite side of the street a few doors along, someone sitting at the wheel. A black Ford Kuga. From where she stood, Lauren couldn't tell whether the driver was male or female; it was already dark, and the person was either wearing a hat or had their hood pulled up. It seemed strange, because she was sure that when she'd got home from work earlier that evening, the same car had been there, the same figure sitting at the wheel. She hadn't thought anything of it then – the car might have just pulled into the street. But now, hours later, it seemed suspicious that someone would still be sitting there; too much of a coincidence that they might have got back into their car just moments before Lauren came out of the flat.

The local convenience store was at the other end of the next street, so she had no reason to walk past the car, not unless she wanted to double the length of her route. Instead, she turned a couple of times as she walked away, waiting to see whether the driver reacted to spotting her. Was the car there for her? Was she stupid even to consider it, allowing her imagination to run wild with ridiculous possibilities? But perhaps they weren't ridiculous at all. Someone knew where she lived and they had targeted her. Perhaps not worrying enough was her biggest problem.

The thought catching hold of her and refusing to be shaken off, she hurried to the shop, bought milk and quickly headed towards home, desperate to be back inside the flat. When she got to her street, the car was gone. She was overthinking everything, she realised; suspicion was making her paranoid. Yet still, her pace slowed as she neared the flat, expecting something else to be there waiting for her when she arrived home. But there was nothing. By the time the door was locked behind her, she had gone off the idea of tea. Finally, she let go of the tears of frustration she had managed to hold in earlier.

The following day would be the four-year anniversary of her mother's death. Each year, the date brought with it the same confusion of emotions, because Lauren wanted to feel the way she suspected most people felt when they marked the passing of a person they had once loved. But she couldn't, not after what she'd found out.

Her mother had always been slight, frail even in her younger years, but she had never looked so small as she had that evening, barely a curve beneath the thin hospice blanket. The nurses had said for days that there wasn't much time left, but

Lauren had known this was the end – she could feel it in her heart, heavy and final. With fingers that trembled despite her attempts to stop them, she had gripped her mother's hand, fearful that the moment she relaxed her grasp would be the moment her mother finally let go of life.

There were things she supposed she was meant to say – words that if left unsaid now would never be spoken – yet she didn't know what they were or where she might find them hidden within herself. Their relationship was complex, as she supposed most were, though for Lauren and her mother, the intricacies were so historic and deep-rooted that there was now no way of them ever being able to get through them. They should have done it all before. They should have had those conversations. Now they had run out of time.

'The roses are looking good, Mum,' she'd said, because in the moment that was all she could think to say, the first distraction that came to mind from all the things she couldn't bring herself to consider. She gestured to the windowsill, where the small wicker basket she had bought for Mother's Day held a tiny bloom of blush-pink petals. 'That bit of water yesterday did them the world of good, didn't it?'

Her mother turned her head towards the flowers, the effort visible with the slowness of her grey skull.

'Maybe I should get another one for the other end, what do you think? Beauty is found in symmetry, so they say.'

And then her mother had spoken her name, her voice barely audible. The sound of it had echoed in the bare room. It had been so long since she had called her by her name. 'Stop.' Her fingers squeezed around Lauren's own. Her pale, watery eyes looked up at her, a last spark of light still apparent in the cool blue of her irises.

'Jamie...'

'Jamie's fine, Mum. I promise.'

Jamie wasn't fine. A fortnight earlier, he had been beaten to within an inch of his life by a couple of fellow inmates who hadn't taken kindly to the fact that he had helped himself to drugs from their cell. He was only a couple of months from release, but that would be too late for their mother to see him. Better for her to think of him as he was before, years earlier, than see him as he was now, a shell of a man hollowed out by drug addiction and a succession of bad choices.

Her mother had gasped suddenly, a sharp intake of breath that had made her chest heave.

'Try to relax, Mum.' Lauren had eased her fingers from her mother's icy grip.

'That night,' her mother said, wheezing with the effort of the words. 'There's something I need to tell you.'

In her tiny flat, four years on, the room chilled around Lauren as it had done that evening. The walls shrank to confine her. She recalled her mother's words and the tone with which they had been spoken; she remembered feeling numb at the sound of the confession. Whatever else she might have expected to pass between them that evening, this was something she had never anticipated, something she could never have prepared for. She felt the onslaught of grief that had crushed her in its landslide that evening so many years ago hit her all over again, as though she was hearing the declaration for the first time.

The sound of her phone broke her from her thoughts, and she pulled it from her pocket. Withheld number. She took it into the living room with her, hesitating before swiping with her thumb and raising the phone to her ear. She said nothing, waiting for the person at the other end to speak. Breathing, clear and distinct. Enough to let her know that someone was there.

'Who is this?' she said, knowing she would get no answer.

The breathing was steady and purposeful. Then, moments later, the call was cut.

Lauren put the phone on the windowsill and grabbed the first thing that came to hand: a ceramic jug that had been part of a gift of flowers from Fiona when she'd been unwell a few years earlier. Her fist closed around the handle, her knuckles white with tension, and when she threw it, a million furies were expelled from her body, quickly replaced by a million more. The jug hit the wall and smashed to pieces over the laminate flooring. She felt no better for it; no worse. She felt nothing.

There was a movement inside her as the baby protested against the noise and the violence. Lauren placed a hand on the swell of her stomach, whispering a slew of apologies, at once remorseful for the rage that had come with her reaction. *You are not her*, she told herself, as she had done so many times before. *You are not a product of what she was.*

Yet the facts remained, and she doubted herself as she tried to quell the voice within her.

Some women just weren't fit to be mothers.

FOURTEEN

THE MIDWIFE

Jackie never stayed overnight at the hotels where she met Peter. When she got into her car after leaving him, she found herself heading away from her flat in Oakwood and soon leaving London. With the radio turned up, she allowed her brain to steer the car where her subconscious wanted to take her. The openness of the M4 felt like an escape, and almost two hours after leaving the B and B, she finally reached home.

Her stomach twisted into a knot as she passed the sign that welcomed her to the village of Purton. The streets were dark and quiet – night had stilled and silenced the place – and as she turned into the street she had once called home, she felt a tug of nostalgia stronger than she had anticipated. She stopped the car opposite the house and turned off the engine. They had been so lucky, she had realised that afterwards. For everything they hadn't had, there was so much that was theirs, yet it hadn't seemed enough to her, not at the time.

The house was a three-bedroom stone cottage in the centre of the village. From the outside it looked modest, but inside it boasted a beautiful living room with a wooden-beamed ceiling. The kitchen ran the width of the back of the house, but the real selling point, and the feature that Jackie had fallen in love with when she and Simon had first viewed it, was the huge garden backing onto open countryside.

The street was quiet, many of the houses submerged in darkness, but there was a light on in her former home, the curtains in the front window framed by the soft glow of the living room. She pictured it as it had been when she'd lived there: the whitewashed walls, the pastel furnishings, the airy feel she had tried to breathe through the building. She wondered what it might look like now. The thought of strangers having changed the place beyond recognition brought a sadness that caught her off guard. A lifetime had been played out beyond that front door; a time that now seemed like a different world altogether. There had been laughter, celebrations, tears and arguments: all the things that formed the backdrop of any home, so much of it taken for granted at the time.

She took a deep breath as she tried to dispel her thoughts. They had been so lucky to live here. It was a chocolate-box location, the kind of place couples worked their entire careers towards, yet it had been Jackie's before she'd reached thirty. Perfect for a family, she thought, and it hit her with a brutality she should have predicted. The second bedroom had been the start, offering a glimpse of what family life might one day look like for them. Instead, the room had eventually been redecorated, the books donated to charity shops, the bedding removed and never replaced. She had never become a mother, relegated to the permanent position of auntie and mum's-best-friend, always there for other people's children whenever they had needed her. It was fine, she was happy, except for the times when she wasn't, times when the loss would feel acute and she would bleed out from within, an invisible injury she carried alone and treated in the only way she knew how, with an outward kindness that at times felt it would kill her.

Instead of a garden filled with children's toys and laughter, a tree had been planted for every loss: four in total. They would remain there for ever, even after she was gone – and she would stay with them until the choice was no longer hers to make. That time had come far sooner than expected. Once the word divorce had been uttered, the damage was irreversible. There had been no way she could afford the mortgage repayments on her own, and buying Simon out of his share was also an impossibility. She dreamed of being able to take the trees with her, but they had grown too big, their roots embedded within the earth. It had been over a decade since she had last seen them.

She got out of the car and locked it. She walked to the end of the row of cottages and headed towards the path that led to the field at the back of them. She stumbled a couple of times in the darkness and had to pause to allow her eyes to adjust, but she knew straight away once she'd reached the back of the garden that had once been hers, spotting the shapes of the trees dancing in the night breeze. In the darkness, it was difficult to make out where one ended and another began, but as her eyes started to adjust and she was able to re-familiarise herself with the layout of the garden, she realised that there were only two there. The others were gone. Her heart fluttered in her chest at the thought of them being chopped down, their roots dug out and disposed of, their remains hacked up and thrown into a wood burner. When she looked further up the garden to the back of the cottage, she saw for the first time the outline of the extension that had been built there, the reason her trees had been culled.

She felt each loss anew, as though she was losing two of her babies all over again. While those trees were still there, they had continued to exist; she had taught herself to imagine her unborn children somewhere, living lives that had been kept apart from her own. They were happy. They were healthy. In some alternative world, they were real. It was the only way she had been able to keep herself going.

Her hands closed into fists at her sides as she tried to hold back a wave of hot and angry tears. She wanted to go to the front of the cottage, to knock on the door and confront whoever was sitting in that living room; she wanted to ask them whether they had any idea of what they'd done, or whether they'd so much as considered the relevance of the trees they had probably hacked down without a second thought.

A single drop of rain hit the side of her face and ran down her cheek. She was shaking. She had to get back to London, and yet she didn't want to leave.

She should never have come here, she thought. If she had never seen the place, she would never have known. Ignorance would have been bliss.

The unfairness of it all caught her in the back of her throat, threatening to choke her. Over the years, Jackie had seen all kinds of mothers: the good, the bad, the undeserving. Of course she wasn't supposed to say so, and she never did, her judgement smothered beneath the professionalism she wore effectively enough to conceal her true thoughts. But the facts remained. Some women didn't deserve to be mothers. So what had she done that was so bad fate had decided she should never be allowed the opportunity?

As she hurried back through the field, the skies opened in a sudden downpour. By the time she reached the car, the thin jacket she'd been wearing was soaked through. She peeled it off and turned on the engine, blasting the heating to cut through the chill that permeated her bones. It wasn't the night air alone that chilled her. She shouldn't be here, she thought. There was someone else who needed her now.

Lauren's baby.

FIFTEEN

THE MOTHER

Lauren's second meeting with Jackie and Amber took place the following week as they had scheduled. It had rained relentlessly all morning, the grey streets a blurred backdrop to the downpour, the roads glistening mirrors reflecting the life that moved reluctantly above. The five-minute walk from the Tube station left Lauren soaked through, her umbrella as good as useless against the tireless wind. By the time she got to the community centre, she was shivering with cold. Jackie was already there, prepping tea and biscuits. Her silver-blonde hair was swept back into a short ponytail at the base of her neck, and she was wearing her standard out-of-work outfit of fitted jeans and sweater.

'Morning.'

She turned at Lauren's voice. 'Oh God, you're soaked through.' She put down the box of tea bags and hurried to help her with her coat. 'Here,' she said, pulling a seat towards the radiator. 'Sit here, you'll soon warm up. They've always got them cranked up high – must cost them a fortune.'

Lauren found herself allowing Jackie to take her coat from her, grateful to be looked after. As she watched Jackie hang her wet coat at the end of the radiator before returning to her arrangements of biscuits on a plate, she wondered whether she was a mother herself. It had never arisen in conversation, though she seemed the maternal type, whatever that was.

'How has your week been?' Jackie asked, as she took a seat opposite Lauren.

Lauren wished she could tell her the truth. If there was anyone she felt she might be able to confide in, Jackie was that person. Though she had known her for so little time, she seemed trustworthy and non-judgemental: the kind of woman Lauren wished her own mother had been. The thought stabbed like a blade edge.

'Fine. Nothing much to report, really. Yours?'

'Busy with work, but nothing new there. I wouldn't have it any other way.'

The door opened, and Amber entered the room. She too was soaking wet, and Lauren watched as Jackie jumped up and took her coat, hanging it up to dry. Why did she put herself to all this voluntary effort when her paid work must already take up so much of her time and energy? She seemed to care more than was required of her, though Lauren supposed it wasn't possible to be too kind. It was sad that it made a person seem suspicious in some way.

'Shall we start with the tea today?' Jackie suggested. 'You both look as though you could do with warming up.'

As Jackie made tea, Lauren asked if they were expecting any of the other mothers who hadn't made it to the session the week before. Jackie told her she wasn't sure.

'It's so informal, and everyone's so busy. Doesn't suit everyone.'

'It's quite nice with just the three of us,' Amber said, taking the cup of tea that Jackie held out for her. When she sat back, she moved a hand to her stomach. Her bump was perfect, Lauren thought; small and neat. Amber seemed to have avoided the weight gain that Lauren was now experiencing elsewhere. She had noticed recently that her face was fuller, and she was definitely carrying more around her hips than she had before.

'I keep thinking about the labour all the time recently,' Amber said, as Jackie handed Lauren a mug and then sat down with her own. 'Not going to lie, I'm bricking it. I might ban my boyfriend from the room, I reckon he'll only make things worse. I know someone who had their dad in the delivery room with them – have you ever heard anything so weird? What about you?' she asked, turning to Lauren. 'You having yours in there with you?'

'My dad?' Lauren asked, with a wry smile.

'No!' Amber laughed. 'Your boyfriend, husband, whatever.' She glanced at Lauren's ring finger. 'Are you married?'

'No. No boyfriend either. Actually, I had IVF with a donor.'

This was something Jackie would already know from Lauren's hospital records, but it had never been spoken about, and it felt good for once to be able to talk to someone. Lauren had never met anyone else who had gone through a pregnancy alone in this way. She waited for a reaction, still wary of possible judgement.

'Good for you,' Amber said. 'Was it painful?'

Jackie flinched at the question, but Lauren appreciated Amber's no-nonsense approach; far better that, she thought, than the kind of women she lived with in the past, the ones who had been one thing to her face and something different behind her back.

'A bit,' she admitted. 'Probably nothing compared to giving birth, though.'

'You'll find out soon enough. How many weeks are you now?'

'Thirty-four. You?'

'Twenty-eight.'

Jackie sipped her tea and listened quietly as the conversation progressed to baby names. Amber was having a boy, she told them, though she was finding it difficult to settle on a name she liked.

'Have you found any you like yet, Lauren?' Jackie asked.

'For a girl, maybe Sophia. And for a boy, I'm not sure. I'm finding it harder to pick a boy's name.'

'See,' Amber said, putting her empty cup on the windowsill behind her. 'Boys are tricky, aren't they? I did think about letting my boyfriend choose it, but God knows what the poor baby would end up with.'

They fell into silence for a moment, and Lauren's thoughts trailed to Callum, as they had done so many times since she had seen him at the shops. She thought of his new girlfriend; his new life. She wondered if he was happy. She hoped he was happy. He had wanted a son; he had told her as much during one of their several conversations about possible parenthood. Maybe that would happen for him soon enough.

'I'm thinking of having a home birth,' Amber said, breaking the silence. 'Have you considered one of those, Lauren?'

'Really?' Jackie said. 'You've not mentioned it before.'

'I've been doing a bit of reading on it. It's a nice idea really, to be at home in your own surroundings.'

'It's not that straightforward,' Jackie told her. 'There are a lot of medical and safety issues to consider. It's Lauren's decision to make, no one else's.'

Lauren noticed the look that shot from Amber to Jackie. It was more than simply questioning; it was hostile.

'All the stories I've read about women who've given birth at home have been positive ones,' Amber continued, directing her words at Lauren.

'What about pain relief?' Lauren said. 'You did say you're bricking it.'

Amber smiled. 'Yeah, there is that. Can't ask for an epidural at home, can I? What about you, though? I reckon you're made of tougher stuff than I am. You'd cope with just a bit of gas and air.'

Lauren looked from Amber to Jackie, whose face had hardened, her mouth set in a thin line. Perhaps she felt Amber was undermining her by talking about something of which she had no experience other than a few internet searches.

'These are decisions you'll both need to make,' Jackie said coolly. 'Would either of you like more tea?'

The atmosphere remained strained for the rest of the session, Jackie unusually quiet while she allowed Amber and Lauren to lead the conversation. At the end, Lauren noticed that Amber left without saying goodbye. Birthing was such an emotive subject and such a personal choice, yet it seemed to create controversy for reasons Lauren couldn't understand. Surely everyone's priority was making sure a child made its arrival into the world safely without the mother's health being compromised.

Lauren was soaked once again by the time she got back to her street. She saw the car – a black Ford Kuga – before she looked at the flat. It was the same one that had been there before; she recognised the number plate. She stopped on the pavement. She didn't want to go back to the flat, not while someone might be there watching it. Watching her. But where would she go? She would have no choice other than to return later, and the car might still be there.

As she stood deliberating, the door to the flat opened. Lauren felt bile rise in her throat as a man came out. Karim. She moved behind a parked car, her heart thumping in her chest. He had gone into her flat without her permission. He had a key; he could let himself in at any time. She crouched behind the car, not wanting to be seen. The baby kicked in protest, and Lauren fought to hold back tears. It felt as though the baby was trying to tell her something. A warning. Just how much did Karim know about her? She had been so stupid, so naïve to think him in any way interested in her when all this time he might have been responsible for tormenting her.

She peered around the car. He was gone. When she stood, so was the black Kuga. She turned and headed away from the flat. She had no idea where she was going or who she might turn to for help; all she knew was that she needed to get away from there.

SIXTEEN

THE MIDWIFE

Before Melissa Parker became a different person, she had lived for a while in a house in Brighton that had been rented by her and three other young women. One of those women, Becky Hargreaves, had drowned during a house party, the police investigation into her death concluding that she had consumed a large amount of alcohol and drugs during the evening and that it had been a case of accidental death. The two other housemates, both now in their mid thirties, had gone on to have successful careers and family lives, one now working in television production and the other, Dawn Beckett, practising as a reflexologist from her home in Ilford.

The drive from London to Ilford had taken Jackie beneath the grey skies forecast to travel towards the city later that day. Threats of a storm had seen people cancel travel plans; the roads were quiet, and she knew she should probably have postponed her visit. Now, sitting in the small but warm wooden cabin that had been built in the garden of Dawn's home to accommodate her clients, her doubts returned to her. She should have stayed home. She shouldn't have come here.

Dawn Beckett was a youthful-looking woman with a freckled

complexion and short-cropped hair. She wore a plain black button-down dress and a pair of flip-flops, despite the nip of winter chill that remained in what should by now have been spring air. Hot-pink nails flashed from her bare toes as her right foot tapped rhythmically on the panelled floor. She sat beside Jackie at the makeshift desk in the corner of the room, rifling through paperwork.

'The boring bit, I'm afraid. Only needs to be done on the first visit. If you could just fill this out,' she said, pointing to the top section of the first sheet, 'and this part, that would be great.'

Jackie answered a series of questions about her health, past illnesses and allergies before handing the forms back to Dawn, who gave them a quick glance before putting them in a drawer.

'Great, thank you. So it's feet and head we're looking at today, is that right? You mentioned in your email that you've been struggling with tension headaches.'

Jackie nodded. 'They're quite sporadic.'

'What job do you do?'

'I'm a teacher,' Jackie said, not wanting to reveal anything about herself. The lie lifted easily from her tongue, though the problem, she knew, was not telling the lies but remembering them all.

'Lots of pressure, then. Right, you get yourself settled on the bed and I'll be back in a minute.'

Dawn left the cabin, leaving Jackie alone. The place was scented with vanilla tea lights, and the lighting was kept dim to create a relaxing atmosphere. Postcards of the sea had been pinned to the ceiling above the treatment bench. Jackie wondered whether Dawn missed living on the coast, though she doubted she missed Brighton, with all the memories it must hold.

She lay on the bench, wondering how she was going to feign relaxation, and a minute or two later, Dawn came back in. She began the treatment by focusing on Jackie's head, speaking only a couple of times, once to ask whether Jackie was comfortable and another to request that she let her know if anything was painful; other than that, the room was silent, and Jackie wondered how and when she was going to be able to raise the subject she had come here to explore.

She should have found herself relaxing as the treatment progressed, yet she couldn't allow herself to. She was fraught with anxiety and with thoughts of Melissa Parker, a woman who was apparently responsible for so much misery and destruction. A woman responsible for murder. Peter was surely right: someone else must have known what had really happened that night. Someone else must have seen through Melissa and realised what she was, and yet if anyone had, they had kept the knowledge to themselves all these years.

When Dawn had finished the treatment to Jackie's head and shoulders, she moved to her feet. Jackie gazed at the seascapes on the ceiling. At last she had an opportunity to speak. She gestured to the postcards pinned above her. 'You like the sea?'

'My favourite place to be.'

'I've always wanted to live on the coast somewhere,' Jackie said. Before Peter had contacted her eight months earlier, it had been her plan to take early retirement and move abroad somewhere. She'd had her sights set on Portugal. 'Have you ever lived by the sea?'

'A long time ago.' Dawn's fingertips pressed gently into Jackie's right sole.

'Whereabouts?' Jackie asked.

'Brighton, when I was younger.'

'Would you ever go back?'

'Not now.'

Jackie wished she was better prepared. She had gone there on a whim, desperate to know more about Melissa Parker.

Dawn had lived with her; surely she would have caught at least a glimpse of the person Melissa really was?

'I used to know someone who lived in Brighton,' she said, trying to sound as casual as she could. 'Her name was Melissa.'

She felt Dawn's reaction in the change of pressure against her foot. When she looked at her, Dawn's face was neutral, her reaction brief and controlled. She was trying to maintain her professionalism, but it was clear the name had struck a nerve. She continued her work silently, as though the name that had just been spoken hadn't sparked any kind of recognition.

'I need to talk to you, Dawn. About Melissa Parker.'

Dawn's hands fell from Jackie's feet and her chair scraped across the floor as she pushed it back. 'Who are you?'

'I'm not here to cause trouble,' Jackie said, sitting up. 'I just need to know what happened that night.'

Dawn's jaw tightened. 'I don't know anything about what happened other than what I told the police at the time. Who are you? Why have you come here?'

'Was Melissa involved in what happened, Dawn? I promise you, I don't want to cause trouble for you. I know Melissa. I just need to know who she really is.'

Dawn reached for her mobile phone on the table. 'I'm calling the police.'

'Don't,' Jackie said, raising a hand. 'I'll go. I'm sorry. I shouldn't have come here.'

She stood and reached for her things, fumbling in her bag for three twenty-pound notes, which she left on the table before apologising again as she left the cabin. She wished she had never gone there. Doing so had offered her nothing, and if Peter were to find out, he would be furious with her. Even worse than the thought of Peter's reaction, though, was the idea that Dawn might still be in contact with Melissa. If she was, Jackie might just have made things worse than they already were.

SEVENTEEN
THE MOTHER

That night, the storm that had been forecast hit London with even greater force than had been anticipated. Lauren spent the first part of the night unable to sleep, watching from the living room window as the trees that lined the street were bent like pipe cleaners by the wind and the litter blown from fallen bins danced erratically along the road and pavement. Despite the fact that the window was newly replaced, the force of the storm was strong enough to rattle it, and there were moments when Lauren felt pressure from behind it, as though once again she would be met with a burst of shattered glass.

She had triple-checked the bolt across the front door, though there wasn't one on the back door. Would Karim have a spare key for that too? she wondered. It seemed more than likely, and the thought had kept her from sleep, enough to make her take a kitchen knife to the bedroom with her that now sat waiting on the bedside table, its presence a reminder that even home was no longer a safe place. A shiver shot through her. It was cold, but she didn't want to put the heating back on. Instead, she got into bed in her dressing gown and pulled the duvet up to her chin, warding off the chill that had seeped into her bones. Exhausted and defeated by fear, she fell in and out of dreams, blurred snapshots of times and places; voices from the past that called out to her, insisting on making themselves heard. She saw Jamie's face. Callum's. Nathaniel's.

She was ripped from sleep at the sight of the boy, his eyes hollowed and darkened, unable to see her in the way she could see him. She felt wetness beneath her, a stickiness between her legs, and smelled the metallic scent of blood. Her heart pounded in her chest so hard it threatened to burst, and it took a moment for her eyes to adjust to the darkness. Her hands fumbled beneath the duvet, searching for the blood in which she lay. But they met with nothing more than the dry sheet, and her heart began to slow with the realisation that it had just been a dream. A nightmare.

Rain battered the window, hammering a relentless beat against the glass that seemed to Lauren a form of torture. She sat up and tried to chase away the ghosts that stood in the room around her, gathered by her bedside. She leaned over and reached for the lamp. The light came on and the ghosts dissolved, leaving her alone. Yet fear remained. Thoughts of Jamie couldn't be shaken. Did Karim know him somehow? If Karim was responsible for putting that newspaper clipping through the door, had he learned from Jamie who she really was? It seemed implausible that the two of them should ever have met, yet she had no way of knowing. She realised she knew nothing about her landlord. Having money meant nothing; Karim might have been to prison in the past, for all she knew. Perhaps that was where he'd met her brother.

She thought of Karim inside the flat. Had he gone through her things? Had he been looking for something? The thought that he may have had time to install a camera somewhere hit her with the force of a punch. She got out of bed and checked the corners of the ceiling, the light fitting, the mirror on the wardrobe door. Not being able to see anything didn't mean it wasn't there. It didn't mean that he couldn't see *her*.

Sick at the thought, she went to the kitchen to get herself a glass of water. Her throat felt dry and sore, and the start of a headache pinched at her temples. She took a deep breath and tried to calm her thoughts. She was being ridiculous, imagining all sorts of scenarios that had no foundation other than her own imagination.

She raised the kitchen blind to assess the damage to the garden, though it was difficult to see in the half-darkness. Though the rain persisted, the wind had dropped and the storm was beginning to subside; by sunrise it would be over, leaving its chaos behind. As her eyes adjusted to a darkness broken only by the glow from the kitchen, she could make out the silhouette of something twisted on the small square of grass. For an awful moment, the darkened shape resembled the outline of a body. Heart pounding in her chest, Lauren went to the back door and braced herself against the downpour.

Her held breath was expelled at the sight of the fallen rotary line, bent and twisted on the lawn. Debris had been blown in from the lane at the back of the garden: a couple of crisp packets caught on the thorns of the potted roses Lauren had tried to revive after finding them neglected when she'd moved into the flat; a torn brown paper bag lying on the muddy ground. But that wasn't all. Something else had caught her eye. At the centre of the grass, not far from the fallen washing line, the ground had been disturbed, and as she got closer, she could see that it had been dug into. A rectangle in the turf. A hole.

She stooped and swiped the loose earth with the palm of her hand, rain running in rivers down her face. The hole was so shallow that its contents were barely concealed. She reached into it, a makeshift grave, and pulled out a box, almost dropping it as she realised what it was. Her heart hammered painfully at the memory of the shredded and bloodied Babygro. The cardboard was soft in her hands, sodden with rain. There was a brand name on the side: a popular make of running trainer. The size was printed beneath it.

A wave of sickness rose from her stomach, and she tasted bile in her mouth. Her hand shook as it hovered over the lid of the box, fear keeping her from lifting it while a macabre curiosity urged her to look inside. The rain was getting heavier again, but she barely felt it. *Don't do this to me*, she pleaded, not knowing who she was speaking to. *Don't do this.*

She pulled off the lid. Inside there was a doll, small and without clothing, its tiny limbs twisted into awkward angles. Its eyelids were lifted so that it was staring straight at her, its cold blue eyes piercing even in the darkness. A shiver ran beneath Lauren's dressing gown, chilling her to the core, and she turned towards the end of the garden, half expecting to see someone standing there, watching her. Finding herself alone, she hurried back into the flat and locked the back door before going to the front to check that it was also secure. She returned to the bedroom and grabbed the used towel that hung on the radiator, lying it on the bed before putting the soiled box on top of it. The doll continued to stare at her, its blue eyes following her wherever she moved.

I see you, they seemed to say. *I know what you did.*

EIGHTEEN

THE MIDWIFE

The antenatal ward was short-staffed, and the timing couldn't have been worse. Three expectant mothers were in the latent phase of labour, one with an infection, all in pain and all needing attention. Jackie had been on her own for much of the afternoon, without the help of a healthcare assistant, the other midwives on shift having to flit between wards. She hadn't been able to take a lunch break, and the headache that had crept up on her that morning had reached a thundering peak by mid afternoon, the pressure at her temples so intense it was distracting.

At 6 p.m., she did a drugs round, giving two of the women the medications noted on their charts. She was hoping that neither would move into active labour until after the next shift arrived in an hour. She would stay to help with the deliveries, but dealing with the current workload on her own was an almost impossible task, and the last thing anyone needed was for both babies to decide they were ready for their arrival into the world.

The second of the two women needed an IV medication that had to be signed off by a checking midwife. Jackie called through to the postnatal ward and waited for another member of staff to arrive. When her colleague finally turned up, she looked fraught and her face was flushed; things were apparently just as hectic over in postnatal as they were here.

'I'm sorry, I got here as quickly as I could. We've got a husband playing up.'

'What do you mean?' Jackie asked.

'Wants us to discharge his wife and baby.' The midwife rolled her eyes. 'Probably a match on he wants to get home in time for.'

Jackie might have laughed if the comment had been implausible. Maternity units brought out the best and worst in people, and in some circumstances, they showed them in their true colours. Jackie had seen everything over the years, from attempted abductions from the maternity wards to newborn babies suffering drug withdrawal from heroin-addicted mothers. Little now surprised her.

The two midwives checked the drug together and added it to the bag of saline. They signed the additive label, identified the correct patient and commenced the infusion. The expectant mother was silent as the medication was administered, though her pain remained visible, her face fixed in a frozen grimace. The silence worried Jackie. The medication didn't yet seem to be having its intended effect, and if the infection became any worse, the woman would need to be sent for a Caesarean.

'That should kick in soon,' she told her, putting a reassuring hand on her arm. 'Try to get some rest if you can.'

The other midwife's phone rang. Jackie watched as she answered, noting the way her jaw clenched. 'I'm on my way back over. Have you called security?'

'What's happened?' Jackie asked.

Her colleague returned her phone to her pocket. She checked the patient beside her and discarded the empty IV bag in the bin.

'That husband's assaulted one of the catering staff.'

'Christ. Is she okay?'

Jackie followed the midwife to the postnatal ward further along the main corridor. When they got there, they could hear a man shouting in one of the end rooms. A young midwife was sitting beside a woman wearing a blue overall who had her hands held to her face, blood seeping between her closed fingers.

'He just went for her,' the midwife said. She was visibly shaken, clearly unprepared for the situation she found herself in. 'She only asked his wife what she wanted for supper.'

'Fuck off!' they heard the husband yell. 'Get your fucking hands off me!'

A moment later, two security guards manhandled him from the room, still hurling expletives as he was grappled through the double doors and out of the ward. The member of staff who had been assaulted looked up and winced in pain. When she lowered her hands, Jackie saw that her face was covered in blood. She suspected a broken nose. The man must have hit her with considerable force, and the poor woman was in shock.

'I'm going to have to get back,' Jackie said apologetically, worried for the well-being of the women in her care. 'Get a wheelchair and call a porter to take her over to A and E. I'll come back after handover, okay?'

When she got back to the antenatal ward, Sandra had already arrived for her shift. Jackie talked her through the patients' progress, as well as telling her what had happened over in postnatal.

'Sounds as though you've had your hands full. You should have called me.'

'You're here now,' Jackie said.

When 7 p.m. arrived, only one woman had progressed to active labour. Jackie knew that despite wanting to help, she couldn't stay any longer; she was exhausted and hadn't eaten anything since leaving the flat at 5.30 that morning. Her head was still pounding and she felt dizzy with dehydration, her eyes burning with tiredness. She would be no use to anyone in her current state.

She went to the office to collect her things. When she checked her phone, she saw a missed call from Peter. She called him back, but there was no answer. She used the toilet and changed out of her uniform, and as she was about to leave the ward, she heard Sandra call her name. Her colleague looked flustered, her face flushed.

'Everything okay?' Jackie asked.

Sandra approached her with an outstretched hand in which she carried a clear plastic bag. When she got closer, Jackie could see her hand shaking.

'I've just given room three the IV drugs she was due at 6 p.m.,' she said.

Jackie's mouth fell open. 'But I already gave them to her.' She didn't need to tell Sandra that; she already knew. The empty bag she was holding was the one that had held the administered medication, the bag the other midwife had thrown in the bin after she'd got that phone call. Before they'd both rushed over to the postnatal unit.

Before they'd both forgotten to sign the prescription chart that would let everyone else know the meds had been given.

'Shit.'

'Jesus Christ, Jackie, I know you've been under pressure, but what the hell were you thinking?'

'A phone call came in—' Jackie started.

'You sign the chart,' Sandra snapped. 'You always sign the chart. How am I supposed to know what's already been done otherwise?'

'Didn't you ask her if she'd already had the medication?'

'The woman is near delirious with pain,' Sandra snapped. 'She probably couldn't tell you what day it is. It's not for the patients to remember, Jackie – it's for you to do your job properly.'

Jackie didn't say anything. There was nothing she could say. The patient had now received a double dose of the prescribed drugs, and Jackie alone was to blame. She might have harmed her. She might have harmed her unborn baby.

NINETEEN

THE MOTHER

On Monday, Lauren called in sick. She hadn't seen her older brother in over six years. The last time they had been in the same room together, he had been given four years in prison; she had listened silently as the sentence had been passed, and watched as he had been led away by the guards, still not man enough to make eye contact with her. It had been another drugs offence, yet one more crime in a string that had earned him a record long enough to hang him. She had promised herself she wasn't going to attend the trial, but the closer it had got, the more curiosity had pulled her towards the place. Perhaps she'd needed to go there to be reminded that what he'd become was not her fault. No one had forced his hand. No one had made him do what he had chosen to.

He'd been given chances to turn his life around and make something of himself, and still he had thrown everything away, forever his own worst enemy. Once he'd started on the drugs – a habit that had developed during his first stint behind bars – his self-destruction barrelled forward at a rate no one was able to stop. Few people had desire strong enough to get in its way. His probation officer, Graham, had been a constant in his life, bound by his role to do what he could to help Jamie get his life on track. But from what Lauren had discerned from their last few conversations, even Graham had now given up on him.

Now, parked a few doors down from the pizza restaurant, the past gathered like a storm in front of her. A nagging voice in her head had persuaded her that seeing him finally after all this time might offer some form of closure. She needed to know whether he was the one doing this to her; if it was some sort of sick vendetta that had arisen from a decades-old resentment. Had he found out somehow that she was expecting a baby? Was this what had driven him to torment her?

And she needed to find out if he knew Karim. She hadn't spoken to the landlord since seeing him leave the flat, though she'd had a missed call from him. She had started to look for alternative places to live, but the thought of moving house so close to giving birth filled her with anxiety. She was going to confront Karim, she just wasn't ready to do it yet. She needed to find another flat first, or she and her child would end up homeless.

She got out of the car and headed for the restaurant. 'Restaurant' turned out to be a generous overstatement: the place was little more than a takeaway, with a couple of plastic tables and accompanying chairs dotted to one side. A huge framed menu hung on the wall next to a large fridge stocked with fizzy drinks and bottled water, and the bored-looking man at the counter barely raised his head when she walked in.

'Is Jamie working?' she asked him.

Much to her annoyance, the man looked her up and down, his lip curled into a sneer. There was nothing she hated more, but now, the curve of her stomach on display beneath her open jacket, she reacted with a resentment that sparked into anger. She wondered whether parenthood would keep her this way, fiercely protective and intolerant of rudeness.

'He's busy,' the man said bluntly. 'Who's asking for him?'

'Tell him it's his sister.'

There was a flicker of a reaction. Perhaps Jamie had never mentioned having a sister, and why would he? Or maybe the man was aware of her and knew too much. Wherever Jamie went and whatever he did, there would be background checks. It would be impossible for him to ever escape his past. She had known the same would apply to her, though without a criminal record it had been easier for her to create a new life. She felt her face begin to colour, and she hated herself for it. She turned and went back to the door, where she idly gazed at the menu as though considering an order. The thought of food made her stomach turn, and the smell that wafted from the kitchen was far from appetising.

A few moments later, Jamie appeared at the kitchen door. A wave of shock rippled through her at his gaunt, grey appearance. He had always been slim, but now he was skinny, his cheekbones hollowed and dark bags circling his eyes. He was wearing jeans that didn't fit him properly, and his hair needed cutting. There was only three years between the two of them, but he looked a decade older than Lauren.

His eyes moved straight to her stomach, and she registered his surprise. He didn't know, she thought, and the notion dispelled a chain of suspicions that had gone there with her.

When their eyes met, neither of them spoke.

'Can she come through?' Jamie eventually asked, turning to the other man, who shrugged a response.

'Five minutes.'

He gestured for her to follow him, and led her through the greasy kitchen, which smelled of burnt cheese and cheap cooking oil. He pulled off his stained apron, rolled it into a ball and threw it onto one of the stainless-steel worktops.

'When's the baby due?' he asked flatly.

'May.'

He nodded as he held the back door open for her, a chivalrous gesture that was entirely unlike him. At the back of the building was a tiny yard that housed a selection of different-coloured bins and a pile of broken boxes that had been there long enough to get rain-soaked. There was barely space for the two of them out there – not with the kind of distance she wished to keep from him, at least – so she backed herself into a corner, careful not to tread on the rotting food waste that had spilled over from one of the bins.

'Bit of a shock,' Jamie said, gesturing towards her stomach. 'How did you know I'd be here, anyway?'

One of his front teeth was missing. The others were brown and chipped, souvenirs of an unhealthy lifestyle and the countless fights he had got himself into over the years.

'Your probation officer.'

'I don't think he's supposed to just give my details out to anyone, is he?'

'I'm your sister.'

He gave her a sidelong glance and raised an eyebrow. 'When it suits.'

It never suits, she thought. She hated what he was doing, trying to make her feel guilty after all this time, still refusing to accept his own responsibility. But she wasn't going to do this to herself. She wasn't going to do it to her baby. Avoid stress, that was what Jackie had advised. So what was she doing here, when nothing good was likely to come of it?

She needed to know the truth. She just wanted to hear him say the words.

Jamie leaned against the brick wall and pulled a packet of cigarettes from his pocket. 'Why are you here?' he asked as he lit one. His thin lips curled at the corners. 'When was the last time we saw each other? So long ago I can't remember. Never sent me a letter, or a cake with a file in it.' He smirked at his own joke, lips stretching wider, but the smile fell immediately from his face. 'What do you want?'

'I need to know something,' she told him. 'About that night.'

His eyes darkened. 'You already know everything. You were there.'

But she hadn't been. Not for all of it, at least. There had been those minutes when she'd been left alone – minutes that might have been hours, given how stretched-out time had felt to her that evening.

'Did Mum ever tell you anything?'

He took a long drag on his cigarette before blowing a stream of smoke into the air between them. 'Anything about what?'

He wasn't going to do this to her. He wouldn't force her to say it. 'Afterwards. After that night, did she tell you what had really happened?'

Ever since that last conversation with their mother, doubt had sat between her and Jamie, a final nail in the coffin in which their relationship would be buried. Did he know? Had he known for all these years and never said a word?

His eyes narrowed. 'You know everything that happened. Why are you bringing all this up now, after all this time – haven't you done enough damage already?'

She kept her focus on him, searching his face for the slightest hint of a lie. But there was nothing. He hadn't known. He didn't know. Though he had been guilty of so many other things over the years, one thing Jamie had never been was a liar. Each time he'd been arrested, he'd never tried to claim he hadn't been there or that he wasn't guilty of what he'd been accused of; instead, his default attempt to excuse his behaviour was always to blame it on someone else, as though he was still a child. *Look what you made me do.* He was a coward, but he wasn't a liar, and in her heart, Lauren felt certain he didn't know.

With this thought in mind, she took her phone from her

pocket. She had searched online for a photograph of Karim, finding one on his business website.

'Know him?' she said, holding the phone out to Jamie.

There was not so much as a flicker of recognition on his face. 'No. Why?'

She held his eye, leaving time for doubt. Jamie didn't flinch.

'What?' he said eventually. 'Come on, who is he then? Father of the kid?'

She felt her lips purse as she returned her phone to her pocket. Jamie didn't know him. So what the hell was going on, and why had Karim shown such an interest in her?

'You seem settled,' she said, with a forced smile. 'I'm glad to see you doing well.'

Jamie scoffed. 'I live in a shitty little bedsit I can't afford to heat and I put toppings on pizzas that cost more than I earn in an hour. That your idea of doing well, is it?'

'It's a start, isn't it? It's better than what you've come from.'

He finished his cigarette and threw the stub on the floor before crushing it beneath his trainer. 'Go home,' he told her. 'Whatever answers you came here for, I don't have them.'

He turned and went back into the kitchen. Lauren followed. She watched her brother as he returned silently to his work, setting about the task of clearing the chaotic worktop. Until the age of fourteen, he had been in all the top sets in his year group. He had excelled at maths and science, starting his GCSE studies earlier than his peers. He might have made so much of his life had it not been for the company he'd kept. Had it not been for their father.

She felt she should say something to him, make some parting gesture that might leave them on different terms, but she didn't know what the right words were or where she might find them.

'Bye, Jamie.'

She waited a moment for him to reply, but he continued

working as though he hadn't heard her. Perhaps he was right, she thought, as she left the restaurant and made her way back to the train station. Maybe he didn't have the answers she was looking for. But if Jamie didn't have them, someone else did, and Lauren had no idea who that person might be.

TWENTY

THE MIDWIFE

On Tuesday, Jackie arrived early to the mums' group and set everything up as usual. She was tired, still smarting from what had happened at work. Guilt and self-analysis had kept her awake the night before. She could have killed a child. How could she forgive herself? This wasn't her. Her job was to protect babies.

Fortunately, nobody had been harmed. The mother had been treated for the double dose of drugs, and a Caesarean had been carried out that morning. The latter was likely to have been the outcome even had the drug error not occurred, but the mother's ability to endure the procedure might have been affected by the double dose of medication she'd been mistakenly given. It was probable she'd take longer than average to recover from the surgery. The error had been reported to the senior midwife on call, and the chief executive had been notified. Jackie was under investigation, as was the other midwife who'd failed to sign the prescription chart.

She should never have gone to Dawn Beckett's house. She couldn't blame her oversight on that alone, but there was no doubt she was allowing personal issues to affect her work.

There were no private and professional boundaries any more; the two were merged, whether she liked the fact or not. Two months at most, she told herself. Lauren's due date was 22 May; the pregnancy would be allowed to go beyond that by no longer than twelve days, at which point she would be induced. Jackie just needed to make it that far. She needed to deliver that baby. But if a decision was made to suspend her until a disciplinary hearing took place, she wouldn't get the chance. Everything would have been for nothing. All would be lost over a stupid mistake.

She had thought about cancelling the group that morning, but decided her absence might draw unwanted attention. She went to the toilets and rearranged her hair. She didn't want to see herself in the mirror. Where once a confident, competent woman had looked back at her, now she was met with the face of a stranger. The lines that crept from the corners of her eyes had deepened into chasms, the loose skin at her cheeks starting a slow sag into jowls. She looked what she was: exhausted and defeated.

But Lauren couldn't see her like this. She couldn't know that anything had happened or that anything was amiss, and the longer Jackie could maintain the pretence, the better.

Five minutes before the session was due to start, her phone rang loudly in her jacket, and when she looked at the screen, she saw that it was Peter. She cut the call. She would ring him back once she'd worked out what she was going to say to him. Whatever he wanted her for, it could wait. He didn't know about the drug error yet, though she was going to have to tell him soon. If she didn't admit to what had happened, he would find out somewhere else. She knew that would only look worse.

Lauren was late, and when she arrived, Jackie was sitting in the hall on her own. She plastered on a smile as fake as Lauren's name and pushed thoughts of work to the back of her mind. Lauren was dressed in a floral maternity dress and a coat that was too small to button up over her bump. Her hair was unusually dishevelled, piled high in a messy bun and in need of washing, and though she wore make-up, it wasn't enough to hide the dark bags beneath her eyes.

'Morning,' she said, filling her voice with a cheer Jackie knew was forced.

'Amber can't make it,' Jackie explained, as she returned her phone to her pocket. 'She's got a migraine.'

'They're the worst,' Lauren said, taking off her coat. 'I've had a few recently. Are they a pregnancy symptom or is it just bad luck?'

'The latter, I think. Were you prone to them before? Pregnancy seems to exacerbate what was already there.'

'On and off.' Lauren glanced at the empty chairs. There was a look of pity on her face. 'None of the others ever came,' she said, gesturing to the seats. 'Seems a shame when you've gone to so much effort.'

'I haven't had to do much really. It's never been a formal thing. It's just good for people to know that we're here if they need us.' Jackie gave Lauren a smile, and noticed the other woman shift uncomfortably. Was she growing suspicious? She was struck by the thought that perhaps someone from the unit had mentioned to Lauren what had happened. Surely no one would be so unprofessional, and it was too soon for gossip to have spread. But what if it had come from another expectant mother, someone who'd been at the unit and might have seen or overheard something? Did Lauren no longer feel secure in her company? Jackie needed to change that. She needed to maintain her trust.

'How do you and Amber know each other?' Lauren asked. 'I meant to ask last week.'

'Just through the hospital, same way I met you.'

'Oh. Right. I don't remember seeing her at the antenatal class.'

'She couldn't make it. Work. She did it online instead.'

'What does she do?' Lauren asked.

'I'm not sure. She mentioned having her own business, but I don't think she said what it was. Okay. Is there anything in particular you'd like to talk about today? We've not really discussed birthing plans yet. What are your thoughts?'

'Get through it with as little pain as possible,' Lauren joked.

'Always a good start. I was thinking, though, have you considered a home birth? Your pregnancy has been textbook, so there's no reason why you couldn't opt for one.'

There was a lengthy pause. Lauren's face spoke a reaction she didn't need to give a voice to: she must have wondered whether Jackie had forgotten the conversation from last week's session. She should have waited a while, Jackie thought; she should have tried to broach the subject with more subtlety.

'I don't know. I don't really know that much about them.'

'There's a woman under our care at the moment who home-birthed with her first child. I'm sure she'd be happy to chat with you about it if you wanted to get someone's personal experience.'

Lauren nodded politely. 'Last week when Amber mentioned it, you didn't seem keen on the idea.'

Jackie smiled. 'I'm not keen on the idea for *her*,' she explained. 'And she knows that now; we've spoken about it since. I know she won't mind me saying that to you. You heard her concerns about pain management. I think hospital's the right choice for Amber, although obviously the decision lies with her.'

'But you think it's something I should consider?'

She nodded. 'I'll get you some information on it.'

Lauren pushed her hair behind her ear and smiled awkwardly. 'Thanks. I just assumed, you know, that it was a bit risky.'

'General misconception. I've delivered several babies at

home over the years and there have never been any complications. The mums were always grateful to have done it, too. There's no place like home, right?'

Once again Lauren's face gave away her reaction to Jackie's words. Home wasn't a safe place, not for her. But she didn't know that Jackie was aware of the fact. Or did she? Had Lauren somehow found out that she knew more about her life than she'd realised? The thought produced a band of sweat at the back of Jackie's neckline. She was losing her grip on a situation in which she needed to remain completely in control.

There was something different about Lauren this morning, something that sat between the two of them, unspoken and oppressive. She was fiddling distractedly with a stray thread that had come loose from the hem of her maternity dress. She knows, Jackie thought. Something's wrong. She knows too much.

'Is everything okay, Lauren? You seem a bit distracted.'

'I'm fine,' Lauren replied, smoothing the loose cotton onto the printed fabric of the dress. 'I mean, not really. I haven't felt the baby move. Things have been a bit hectic the past couple of weeks, so I wasn't sure at first whether it was just a case of being busy and not noticing the movements. But I've been monitoring it since last night and there's been nothing.' The hand that had smoothed the dress moved to rest on the swell of her stomach. A guilty look had fallen upon her face, as though she felt she might be judged.

'Okay. We need to get that checked out. Can you call the unit and ask to book in a scan? Tell them you've already spoken to me about it.'

'Is it normal not to feel the baby move?'

'Try not to worry.'

It wasn't the answer Lauren had wanted. Her face contorted from guilt to panic, Jackie's words failing to offer any reassurance.

'Will I see you there?' she asked.

She still had her onside, Jackie thought. Lauren still trusted her. More than that, it seemed that she actively needed her.

'Depends when it is. Ask them to get you in this afternoon, and I'll make sure I'm there.'

'Really? Are you on shift later?'

'Yes,' Jackie replied, realising she would now have to find a way to cover the lie. How was she going to explain to her colleagues why she was in uniform on her day off? If she offered to help at the unit outside of her work hours, that could surely only go in her favour. The other staff would think she was trying to make amends for her mistake. Besides, she'd already had to tell bigger lies than this.

'Can I ask you something?' Lauren said. 'Why have you been so nice to me?'

Jackie laughed anxiously, her nerves set on edge by her own trilled response. 'I wasn't aware I'd done anything out of the ordinary. It's part of my job description, isn't it? To care.'

'I know, but at the group with Amber, when she was talking about home births, you just seemed particularly defensive. It isn't a criticism,' Lauren added.

Jackie shifted in her chair, awkward in the spotlight of the other woman's focus. Perhaps being a liar made it easier to spot the same trait in others, an invisible bond that acted as a magnetic field between culprits. They were more alike than Lauren realised; or perhaps she did realise. If so, Jackie had a problem.

'I appreciate your concern for me,' Lauren said, her words strangely formal.

She was losing her, Jackie thought. Lauren knew that her midwife wasn't what she seemed.

TWENTY-ONE

THE MOTHER

In the hours that followed, Lauren tortured herself with the thought that something had happened to her baby. She went home for a while and lay on her bed in the silence of the flat, all her focus channelled on the life that existed within her. She tried to relax, knowing that that way she might have a better chance of sensing any movement. But it was impossible to stay calm when her body was a coiled spring, wound up by the events of the past few weeks. She couldn't stop thinking about the doll in the shoebox that was still sitting at the bottom of the wardrobe. The hole in the ground. Karim. Her brother. Her mother.

After a late lunch, she caught the 28 bus to Lansdowne Road, from where she would make the quarter-hour walk to the hospital. She took the shoebox with her in a carrier bag, disposing of it in a bin near the bus stop. It's just a doll, she tried to tell herself, but what it represented ran far deeper. Getting rid of it had felt sinful somehow, as though in rejecting the item she might be cursing her own future. Her child's future.

No matter how she tried to explain it otherwise, the thought that it had been Karim who'd left the box in the garden refused to stop taunting her. She had seen him leaving the flat. He'd had plenty of time while she'd been at the prenatal group to dig a hole and bury it, but why would he want to? She hadn't yet confronted him about why he'd been there, too scared of what he might be capable of. She kept the door bolted and the kitchen knife by her bedside, but how long those things were going to be enough to keep her safe she didn't know.

The journey to the hospital was starting to feel longer each time, and the more she thought about the distance and the fact that she didn't own a car, the more anxious she was becoming about going into labour. She'd heard stories of husbands and boyfriends having to deliver babies on kitchen floors and in cars at the roadside; the thought of it happening while she was on a train or a bus surrounded by strangers was a prospect that filled her with horror. There were few people she could call upon in an emergency, although she suspected that when it came to it, she might not be too choosy about who was available to help her.

While she was still on the bus, her phone began to ring. The bus was busy, and despite having a seat at the back, Lauren felt wedged between the people either side of her. She opened her bag and glanced at the screen. Withheld number. She pressed the side of the phone and muted the call. She wouldn't answer them any more. If it was Jamie making the calls, he would eventually get bored, yet even as she tried to convince herself that was the case, she feared it wouldn't happen. The brick, the newspaper article, the shredded clothes; the doll in the shoebox. The calls. They were all the same person, of that much she felt sure. Someone capable of tormenting her with such persistence would never just stop because they'd grown tired of their efforts. The chase wouldn't be over until they'd won, their opponent removed from the game.

The thought brought with it a wave of sickness that swept through her in a hot rush. She leaned forward, an involuntary retch escaping her as she held the nausea down. The woman to her right glared disapprovingly over her paperback before moving her feet, seemingly fearful that Lauren might throw up over her boots. She managed to keep the sickness down, even when the bus stopped sharply. When she got up, it seemed everyone else was getting off at the same stop, and a crush of people carried her out on to the road. The open air and sudden space felt more of a threat than a comfort. Someone was watching her, and their intentions went further than psychological torment. That person wanted to hurt her.

She flagged a taxi to the hospital, exhausted by anxiety. In the waiting room of the maternity unit, she idly browsed one of the magazines left on the side table. *Achieve Your Pre-Pregnancy Weight Without Dieting* one headline screamed at her, and she rolled her eyes as she shoved the magazine to the bottom of the pile, sparing the next woman who would sit there the irritation of being exposed to such inane content.

'Lauren Coleman.'

Jackie's voice called her. Lauren got up and followed her down the corridor to one of the scanning rooms. The midwife was dressed in her own clothes, the same as she'd been wearing that morning: jeans and a thin grey sweater that hugged her narrow frame.

'How are you feeling now? I hope you haven't spent all afternoon worrying. Easy for me to say, I know.' She ushered Lauren into the room and closed the door behind her. 'Have you brought your notes?'

Lauren reached into her bag and pulled out the file with her pregnancy records.

'Jump up onto the bed and I'll be with you in a minute.'

Jackie went to the table at the side of the room and stood with her back to Lauren as she checked over her notes. As she waited, Lauren took in the details of the room: the sterile surfaces and the clinical smell of the place. Before today, there had been something comforting in the surroundings of the hospital, the feeling of being close to medical professionals and pain relief offering much-needed reassurance. Now, she found all the steel and the greyness unnerving.

'Okay. Let's take a look at little one.'

Jackie rubbed some cold jelly on Lauren's stomach and applied the audio ultrasound to her skin. 'Try to relax if you can.'

Lauren put her head back and stared at the ceiling as she waited. The wait went on for too long. She felt the Sonicaid move over her stomach, side to side, up and down, as Jackie tried to pick up a heartbeat, but there was nothing.

Then the door opened, and another midwife came into the room. 'Oh,' she said, her eyes narrowing when she saw Jackie. 'You're not on shift today.'

'No,' Jackie said, 'but I've spoken with Sandra. She knows I'm here.'

She smiled at her colleague, but it was unreciprocated. 'I thought I was taking this appointment.'

'Can Jackie do it?' Lauren asked. 'I'm sorry, I don't mean to offend you. It's just that Jackie knows my concerns, and...' She wasn't sure how to finish the sentence without causing any further offence, so she stopped speaking. The midwife's cheeks had flushed pink, and her lips thinned as she looked from Lauren to Jackie.

'Okay. Well... I'm next door if you need me.'

Jackie waited until the other midwife had left. 'Okay,' she said calmly, 'let's try again.' She had a way of doing this, Lauren thought, of sensing her increasing panic and trying to dispel it with a smile or a gentle word of reassurance. Empathy should be natural for someone in the medical profession, and yet Lauren knew from experience that no amount of qualifications could equip someone with the humanity needed for patient-facing roles.

Jackie removed the ultrasound and placed a hand on Lauren's stomach, pushing her fingers firmly into her side. 'Sorry,' she said, sensing Lauren flinch. 'Just trying to wake baby up.'

Something about her words sent a chill through Lauren. She closed her eyes as Jackie once again pressed her fingertips into her skin, the sensation more painful than she feared it was supposed to be. The visions behind her eyelids made her snap them back open. Jackie worked the ultrasound across her stomach again, her face etched with a concern she couldn't hide.

And then they heard the heartbeat. Solid. Regular.

'There we are,' she said. 'Strong and healthy.' They continued to listen as Jackie monitored the heart rate. 'The baby's quite far back. Your placenta may be round at the front – we'll need to take a look on the screen.'

'Is that a problem?' Lauren asked, panic filling her chest.

'Not at all. It's quite common. We'll just have to keep a check that it doesn't block the cervix.' Jackie put a hand on her arm. 'You're worried and that's normal, but you've got to stop doing this to yourself. Everything's going to be fine. The baby was probably in an awkward position yesterday, that's why you haven't felt anything. Maybe it was having a duvet day.' She gave her a reassuring smile. 'Let's take a look, shall we?'

Lauren rested on an elbow as Jackie brought the screen to life on the wall in front of her. Moments later, her child appeared, a soft blur of light and shade. She could make out the curve of the skull, a bent left leg, a right hand raised as though waving to her. She felt a swell of relief and a rush of love that swept through her with an unprecedented sadness.

'There you go,' Jackie said, passing a finger across the screen. She paused on an unidentifiable sepia mass that for all Lauren was able to decipher might have been a kidney or a twin. 'As suspected. Placenta at the front.'

Lauren exhaled too noisily, her relief audible and almost

tangible in the air between them. All she could take in was that the baby was fine, there and waiting to make its entrance into the world. She had to make sure he or she was going to emerge into a safe one, though how she was going to do that, she didn't yet know. How could she keep her history hidden? Her son or daughter would reach an age when they began to ask questions, and lying to her own child would be very different to lying to the rest of the world.

'Here,' Jackie said, passing her a handful of tissues to wipe her stomach with.

'Thank you.'

'Have you thought any more about what we talked about, about a home birth? I mean, it would depend now on how that placenta's looking nearer to your due date, but if everything remains as it is, it'll still be an option for you.'

'I can't. I know you said there's no risk, but I think I'd feel better being at the hospital.'

'Have you even given it proper consideration?' Jackie snapped.

There was a moment of awkward silence. Jackie's face was flushed, though Lauren couldn't tell whether from anger or embarrassment. It was unprofessional for her to be talking to anyone in such a way, and if Lauren wasn't so stunned by the reaction, she might have felt tempted to remind her of the fact.

'I'm sorry.' Jackie smiled, but it was forced. 'It's your choice, obviously.' There was something behind the words, something more than was being said. Lauren felt she should understand what, but she couldn't read Jackie's expression any more than she was able to decipher the words left unspoken. Why was this woman so keen to push the idea of a home birth on to her? It felt more than just a case of giving her options: Jackie seemed to be trying to actively encourage it. Where Lauren chose to have her baby shouldn't mean anything to Jackie, so why had she looked so disappointed when Lauren told her she wanted to deliver at the hospital?

She was being paranoid, she thought. This was Karim's fault. Jamie's. She was becoming so suspicious of everyone that she was even starting to question the midwife's motives. She closed her eyes for a moment as she tried to fight off the mistrust that had seeped into her. It was unfair, she told herself, yet a second voice responded with an echo that told her the doubt was justified.

TWENTY-TWO

THE MIDWIFE

The bottle of wine Jackie had bought from the off-licence two streets away remained in a carrier bag on the floor beside the bed, unopened. Neither of them ever drank much alcohol, and they never drank together. Peter never knew when he might get called away, and Jackie always needed to drive home. They both needed to be alert and ready, always. She didn't know why she'd bought it. She supposed she'd just wanted to feel normal for an evening, or to seem like any other guest, if only to the member of staff she'd had to check in with; to feel as though they were just like any other couple spending a night together at a hotel. She wanted to forget about what had happened at the hospital and at Dawn Beckett's house. For just one evening, she wanted to forget that everything was about to unravel.

Instead, she sat on the edge of the uncomfortable bed sipping the coffee Peter had made her – a disgusting brand of cheap instant from a sachet, made not even marginally more digestible by the dribble of long-life milk he'd drained from a plastic carton. Peter stood at the window as he tapped out a text message. His daughter had tried calling him ten minutes earlier. Jackie had offered to go outside so he could call her back, but he'd shaken his head, rejecting the offer. The guilt that had been born thirty years earlier had grown into something neither of them could be parted from, a shared offspring for which they had joint custody.

Jackie had met his daughter, a pretty and successful woman in her mid thirties who ran a theatre company for teenagers. She was married to a head teacher and they had two young sons. She had remained close to her father, she and her brother still ignorant of the on-off relationship Peter had had with Jackie over the years. Though Peter's marriage had broken down years earlier, Jackie never had any involvement with his family. She was happy to remain separate from that part of his life, yet there had been moments when she'd felt a resentment that ran deeper than she'd been prepared for.

She reached across to the bedside table and put down her coffee cup, abandoning the thin dregs that remained. 'I went to see Dawn Beckett.'

He put his phone on the windowsill and turned to her. She watched as it took a moment for the name to register. 'You did what?'

'I just wanted to find out more about what happened that night.'

'Christ, Jackie, you shouldn't have done that. What did you say to her? Did she know who you were?'

'No. I didn't tell her anything. I gave a false name.' She wasn't going to tell him about how her visit had ended. Some details were best kept unshared.

Peter's mouth set in a firm line. 'You could have jeopardised everything. What if Melissa finds out you went there?'

'How would she? Look, I'm pretty sure the two of them are no longer in contact, if Dawn's reaction was anything to go by.'

'Pretty sure? I don't work on the basis of "pretty sure".'

His tone was so scathing that Jackie felt herself flinch. She wouldn't be made to feel like this again, like the naïve young woman who had faced his animosity all those years ago. They were equals now. He needed her.

He crossed the room and sat beside her. 'I know you don't want to believe that any of this is true.'

Jackie couldn't meet his eye. If he knew the error she'd made at work, she doubted he would even have been in that room with her. There was a chance it could ruin everything. She would put it right and he would never have to know. She couldn't let him down.

'I just... it's hard to believe this is really her. You're describing a different person.'

'This is what she does,' Peter said emphatically. 'She turns people against each other. Makes them doubt themselves. I mean, how could anyone think such terrible things of such a lovely woman? Such a tragic background, such a sad story. She's the victim, isn't she? Not the perpetrator. We should take pity on her. We should feel sorry for her. That's what she wants you to think, because while you're thinking the best of her, she can get away with murder.'

Jackie put her head in her hands. She absorbed every word, though she still didn't want to hear any of them. What he'd said was right. Melissa *was* lovely. She *was* a victim. But she was also someone who was capable of appearing one thing while being something very different, and Jackie knew that a personal tragedy didn't make her innocent. And yet there was still that part of her that didn't want to believe any of it to be true.

'Don't you trust me?' His words were cold. He was offended by the suggestion that had sprung from her doubt; that after all this time of knowing one another, she could still throw into question his integrity and his ability.

'I wouldn't be here if I didn't trust you,' she replied defensively.

'Yet you still went and visited Dawn Beckett without speaking to me about it first. You do your job and let me do mine. Maybe I shouldn't trust *you*, Jackie. You've kept things covered up in the past – there's no reason you shouldn't do it again, is there? If you want to believe Melissa is an innocent victim who needs your help, you go ahead. Forget all of this. Just don't drag anyone else into your mistake. I risked losing everything for you once. I'm not prepared to do it again.'

Jackie got up from the bed and took her bag and jacket from the chair at the dressing table. Peter didn't say anything to try and stop her. 'I'm sorry you feel that way,' she said, trying to steady her shaking voice. 'But you need me more than I need you at the moment. It's me putting everything on the line now, not you. Perhaps you should remember that.'

After leaving the B and B, Jackie headed towards Palmers Green. She found herself driving without concentrating on where she was going, her subconscious navigating her route as it took her closer to Lauren Coleman's flat. The light was on in the living room, and the curtains had been left partly open. There was a flicker of light from the television, though there seemed to be no one in the room watching it. Jackie cut the engine and pushed her head against the headrest. She checked her phone. Peter hadn't messaged her. But he would, she knew. Like she'd told him, he needed her. There had been a time when she'd thought she needed him, but that was no longer the case.

She was pulled from her thoughts by a movement at the window. Lauren wore a pale blue dressing gown knotted around her bump. Her hair was loose, resting on her shoulders in limp curls, recently washed. She didn't see Jackie watching her; she didn't look out onto the street. Her eyes on something else, she reached up to yank the curtains together, blocking out the outside world. A solitary lifestyle, Jackie mused. She wondered if this was how Lauren had lived her entire life, cut off from everyone around her. Her isolation seemed voluntary, though circumstances had helped to dictate the life she would go on to lead.

Jackie reached for the glove box and retrieved the photograph she'd left there weeks ago. The woman's face smiled back at her – one hand raised in an awkward wave at the camera, the other resting on her rounded stomach. Jackie pressed her fingertips to her eyelids as she tried to ward off the sadness that swept through her.

'I'm doing this for you,' she said, as she ran her thumb across the image. 'For both of you.'

TWENTY-THREE

THE MOTHER

The headache that had plagued Lauren throughout that afternoon stayed with her long into the evening, squeezing at her temples. She had spent the day trying to avoid her thoughts, as though they might in some way be escaped if she was only able to distract herself enough. She felt reassured by the scan that afternoon, but it wasn't enough to stop the fears that had consumed her, fears that seemed now to have gathered in the flat to torment her. She was going to have to speak to Karim and find out what was going on.

Stronger than the thought of how Karim might have found out her secret was the worry that there was something wrong with her baby. It wouldn't leave her alone, and the tighter the notion circled, the faster it took hold as a fate that couldn't be avoided. The doll in the shoebox. The hole in the ground. A grave. The scan was false hope; a cruel joke given that it was obvious her life would be plagued by heartbreak. The baby was well, for now. But something was going to happen. She had seen her child with its hand raised, waving. What if it had been waving goodbye? She tried to calm her spiralling thoughts with Jackie's words, but they only worked for so long.

She got up and went to the bedside table, to the top drawer where she'd put the crumpled newspaper article posted through the door. She wished now that she'd thrown it out, destroyed it as she had the note wrapped around the brick. She unfolded and smoothed it out with shaking hands, knowing what would face her.

TEENAGER BEATEN AND LEFT TO DIE

The words brought tears to her eyes, even after all this time. She tried to fight back the memory that had trapped her in its snare. The woman's grimace. The anger that flared in her face; the pain that drew tracks across her features. And worse: the empty deadness that lay behind her eyes.

She scrunched the paper in her fist and took it to the kitchen. She turned on one of the burners on the gas hob and held the article over the flame, watching as the words fell to ash on the steel top. The flame licked her fingertips as the paper burned to its final corner. She dropped it and watched it reduce to nothing before cleaning up the mess that had been left. It felt like a sin, a betrayal. She was hurting him all over again.

She went back to the bedroom and got beneath the duvet, wrapping it around herself to stave off the cold. Her body shook with the chill that gripped her. Eventually she fell into sleep. She found herself in a bathroom, though its details were blurred and indistinguishable amid the pain that ripped through her, tearing through her abdomen and pressing on her insides, a fist crushing her internal organs. She was dying, she thought. This must be what dying felt like. There were sounds around her, panicked voices and crying, though they too were muted, as though she was hearing them from underwater. There was a pain deep in her groin, and when she looked down, she saw the bright blood that stained the lino beneath her, smeared across her palms where she had grasped her own thighs, skin red and livid.

The image ripped her from her sleep. With a thundering heart and a trail of sweat that ran from her neck to her spine, she groped for the lamp on the bedside table and flicked the room into brightness. The shadows that had haunted her sleep were drowned in colour, though they still existed, simply hidden in the artificial lighting.

She pushed aside the duvet to check the sheet beneath her. It was clean. No blood. Everything was as it should have been. She gulped down air as she tried to calm her racing heart. *The baby is fine*, she repeated to herself. *You are fine*. All the talk of home births had settled into her consciousness; she was doing what she always did, imagining the worst and then allowing it to take up residence. Avoid stress, Jackie had advised. Lauren felt an acidic bitterness creep into her at the thought. How could she possibly avoid stress when it was embedded within her, a part of who she was? She carried it like an extra organ, forever aware of its presence. It didn't matter that she had brought it on herself.

In the darkness, all the bad things came back to her, nightmarish in their intensity. A news report, a shoebox, a death. Everything looked worse in the cold and lonely hours of early morning, and yet nothing could look as terrifying as this did. Lauren fought against her thoughts, pleading with them for respite. Sleep came once again, eventually, but it was restless and disturbed. Hellish visions seared through her brain, every doubt and fear gathering to form a tirade of persecution against her.

She was woken by a noise, or it might have been a noise but she wasn't sure if she had dreamed it. A rattling, a clanging... it had been so distant, she couldn't be sure. She lay and stared at the ceiling, letting her eyes adjust to the darkness, and as her other senses wakened, she realised she could smell something.

She sat up, unsure whether this too was a remnant of the dream. But there was no mistake. She *could* smell something. She could smell smoke.

She pushed aside the duvet, reached for the kitchen knife on the bedside table and went to the bedroom door. When she opened it, the end of the corridor was lit by a pale orange glow that seeped from the outline of the kitchen doorway. Then she heard the noise, sparking and crackling, and she realised with horror that there was a fire in the flat. Another noise followed, something indistinguishable from the other side of the door. There was somebody in the kitchen. With her body seeming to act as a separate self, she moved through the hallway, heart racing at the sound of the flames that lapped at the other side of the door. She kicked it open, and a surge of light and heat burst towards her.

TWENTY-FOUR

THE MIDWIFE

Jackie had the day off work, with few other plans than to tidy the flat, do some food shopping and try to avoid the repetition of her thoughts. She had been away from home so much in the past few weeks that the flat had become a dumping ground, and she'd had little time for domestic chores. Now, looking at the chaos that surrounded her, she wished she'd stayed at the hotel with Peter, if only to escape the mess of this place.

Thoughts of the drug administration oversight she had been responsible for had kept her from sleep the previous evening. She had already received an email from work regarding the investigation. Both she and the other midwife involved had been informed that they would need to complete a written statement, reflecting upon the mistakes that had been made and what could be learned from them for future practice. They would also need to meet with the patient for a formal meeting. She should have been relieved that the incident wasn't being taken any further and that a professional conduct hearing hadn't been mentioned, but she was unable to focus on much beyond the fact that the error had been made in the first place.

She sat down at the small folding kitchen table to begin her statement, but soon found herself distracted from the task in hand. There was something else she needed to get down on paper, and until it was done, she knew she would be unable to concentrate on anything else.

Dear Melissa, she began. *I want you to know that the past couple of months haven't been as they may have seemed. I know that you have trusted me, and that I didn't deserve that trust. By the time you read this, the truth will already be out. I need you to know that despite everything, I wish you no harm. I have done what I thought was for the best. My job is to make sure babies enter this world safely. This has remained my focus.*

She stopped writing. The words were wrong. It was all too formal. It sounded like an apology, and that was the last thing she intended. She moved her focus to the laptop and went to the internet search engine. Typing in the name Melissa Parker, she began to scroll through the thousands of results it threw up. She wouldn't find what she was looking for, she already knew that, and yet she still continued to hope that somewhere, at some point, there would be something to support Peter's conviction. So far, that hope remained futile. Melissa had been protected, kept anonymous throughout.

She started to write again. *Dear Melissa, I can't bring myself to hate you, but I hate what you've done.*

She dropped the pen on the table. She could barely find a beginning for the things that needed to be said. She felt she was owed an explanation, as absurd as it might seem to any outsider. It was Melissa who should be explaining herself. Melissa was the one who needed to justify her actions, if such a thing was even possible. Maybe she couldn't, or perhaps she would never feel that it should be expected of her. Perhaps to her mind she had never done anything wrong. If so, that was the most terrifying thing of all.

On the table beside her, her phone pinged with a text message. It was from Peter.

Lauren's flat was set on fire last night.

TWENTY-FIVE

THE MOTHER

Lauren had called 999 before going to the door of the upstairs flat to wake the couple who lived there. The three of them had waited in the street for the fire crew to arrive, the neighbour giving her his jacket since she'd fled the flat with nothing. His girlfriend had been silent and sullen, shivering in her dressing gown and cursing repeatedly beneath her breath. She barely looked at Lauren, presumably blaming her for the fire that had driven them from their home. She *was* responsible; she just didn't yet know how or why.

Despite everything, she was lucky – she tried to remind herself of that. She might have been sleeping. Presumably that was what the person who'd started the fire had been hoping: that she would be in bed, asleep, and would never wake up. Had they wished the same on her unborn child? Who could be sick enough or vengeful enough to want to harm an innocent baby? Karim had seemed so nice, yet there were plenty of examples to prove that face value meant little. Jamie knew now that she was pregnant, but surely even he wasn't capable of this. The doll in the shoebox returned to her like a vision from a nightmare. She was glad she had got rid of it, grateful that she wouldn't have to explain it to the fire investigation team or the police.

Whoever was responsible, there had been no one there when she'd kicked the kitchen door open. The noises of the fire and the echoes of her own dreams had played tricks on her mind, luring her closer to danger; now, safely outside, Lauren chastised herself for putting her baby and herself at risk. Even after the fire was out, she had continued to smell the smoke that lingered in her hair and on her clothes. It had embedded itself in the walls of the flat, tainting everything. The sight of the scorched walls of the hallway and the charred kitchen door that had been shut by the fire crew to conceal the damage that lay beyond remained with her even after she'd been taken to the police station. It ran deeper than aesthetics. The flat had been invaded yet again, her privacy violated. She would never be able to call this place home again.

At the police station, an officer brought her a cup of tea before showing her to an interview room. 'Do you want to make a call?' he asked.

'I've got my phone,' she said, tapping her pyjama pocket, though she had no idea who she'd be able to contact for help. 'When will I be able to get my things? I'll need some clothes.'

'There'll have to be an investigation into how the fire started first,' the officer explained. 'We can get you anything that's not been damaged then.'

'Thank you.'

The officer left her alone. She sipped the weak, watery tea, her stomach growling in protest. Even the baby seemed not to appreciate it. She was going to be asked questions, she thought. Was there anyone she'd had a disagreement with? Anyone she could think of who might wish her harm? Eventually she was going to have to open the Pandora's box of secrets she'd worked so hard to conceal. Once that happened, her life as she had known it for all these years would be over.

She hadn't wanted to admit to either of the officers that there was no one to come and get her. What was she going to do – she could hardly go home on a bus in her pyjamas. She idly scrolled her contacts. Callum? God, no. He would help her, she knew he would; despite everything that had happened between them, he was a good man, and he wouldn't leave her stranded if he knew what had happened. She just didn't want him to know. She couldn't call her boss; Fiona lived forty minutes' drive away, and Lauren would be forced to explain everything that had been going on. Jackie? Completely inappropriate. Karim? She was hardly likely to call him when a part of her suspected he might be involved in some way.

She scrolled back up the list of contacts, her thumb resting over Callum's name. She checked the time. It was past 8 a.m. It seemed she had little other choice.

He answered after just a couple of rings. 'Lauren?'

'I'm sorry to call you. I... I didn't know who else to ask.'

'What's the matter? Has something happened?'

'There's been a fire at the flat. I'm at the police station in Wood Green. I'm so sorry for calling you.'

'I'll be straight there. Are you okay? Is the baby okay?'

Lauren felt her heart heave with his concern. It was such an unfamiliar sensation, to have someone care about her well-being. She had spent the past decade existing, living a life of work and routine, her few friends moving on to families and promotions. 'We're both fine. It was lucky that I woke up.'

'I'm going to come and get you, okay?'

'Thank you. Please don't rush – the police haven't taken a statement from me yet. I'll cover your petrol.'

'I don't care about the petrol.'

He was being too nice, she thought; nicer than she deserved. She thanked him again and hung up, and a moment later the officer who had brought her the tea returned.

'How are you feeling? You must be shaken up.'

'I'm okay.'

'We've just had a call from the fire investigation team. The preliminary examination indicates the fire might have been started deliberately. Do you know anyone who might be responsible? Any disputes with anyone? Anything you can think of, no matter how small it might be, could be useful.'

'I'm sorry,' she said, swallowing down the truth. 'I can't think of anyone. I don't really know anyone in London other than the people I work with.'

This was something she was going to have to sort out on her own. Telling the police would mean exposing herself, and she couldn't go through all that again. Presumably whoever was responsible already knew that her shame would ensure their protection.

'Okay. We'll need to take a formal statement. Did you manage to get hold of someone?'

Lauren nodded. She waited as the statement was written before signing it, then went to the reception area to find Callum. When she got there, someone else was waiting for her. Karim.

'What are you doing here?' she asked, her voice laced with suspicion.

'I got a call from one of the neighbours. Are you okay? You should have rung me.'

One of the neighbours, Lauren thought. A likely story.

'You all right, miss?' A police officer stood behind her. She looked back at Karim and studied him for a moment, hoping he would realise that the look meant she was on to him.

'Fine,' she said. 'Thank you.'

She stepped out of the automatic doors and stopped at the bottom of the steps. Karim had followed her out. 'Why were you in the flat?'

She was safe to ask it here: he was hardly likely to do anything to her outside the police station. She would have to deal with the repercussions later, though the fire meant she wouldn't be returning to the flat now anyway.

'What?'

'I saw you coming out of the flat a couple of weeks ago. Why were you in there?'

His eyes narrowed. 'I left you a voicemail. Didn't you get it?'

Lauren couldn't remember the last time she had checked her answerphone. There had been too much going on, and with all the nuisance calls she'd been getting, she had turned her notifications off.

'The boiler needed a service,' Karim explained. 'It was my fault, it shouldn't have been left so late, but I needed to submit the paperwork for my landlord insurance, so I had to get it done that week. My ex-wife's been in hospital... my mind's been on other things. I did ask if you could let me know if it was a problem.'

She didn't believe it, and he could see it. She reached for her phone and went to her voicemail, her cheeks flushing when she heard the message he'd left over a fortnight earlier.

'So where was he then? The man who did the service? I only saw you leave.'

'I was on the phone to my brother for a while after he went. I hadn't heard from you, so I assumed it was okay for us to go in. I just thought you'd been too busy to get back to me. Look.' Karim tapped his phone screen for a moment before holding it out to her. It was the website of a gas engineer. 'Call him,' he said. 'He'll tell you he was there.'

'Lauren?'

She turned at the sound of Callum's voice.

'Are you okay?' He eyed Karim warily.

'Fine,' she said. 'I just...' She looked from one man to the other, not sure what she should do. Callum had come all this way to get her, yet now she feared she'd made a mistake with Karim.

'Do you still need a lift?' Callum asked.

'Yes. Please.' She turned to Karim. 'Send me your address. I'll come to yours later.'

In the car, she explained to Callum that Karim was her landlord, unsure why she'd felt the need to tell him.

'How did the fire start, do they know yet?'

'Too soon to say.' She wasn't going to tell him it had been started deliberately. Calling him to the station had been a mistake, one she wouldn't have made if she'd only known why Karim had been at the flat that day. If she hadn't let her suspicions run wild.

'Where am I taking you?'

Lauren had no idea. 'A supermarket, please. Can't spend the rest of the day in my pyjamas, can I?' She looked out of the window, embarrassed.

Her thoughts returned to the doll in the shoebox. The same person who'd put it there must have started the fire, there was little doubt of that. All she had to do was find out who, and why.

TWENTY-SIX

THE MIDWIFE

Jackie had to grip the steering wheel to stop her hands from shaking. She had hurriedly gulped down a black coffee before leaving the flat, needing the rush of caffeine to prompt her leaden body into catching up with her wired brain. Peter's text had sent her mind spiralling. How had he found out about the fire so quickly? It was his job to find out, she answered herself. If he hadn't, he wouldn't be particularly good at what he did. This was exactly what made him credible. The very reason she should believe every word he said.

She had sent a text before leaving the flat, her hands shaking as she'd typed the message.

Meet me at the rose garden in High Barnet Park. I need to see you.

Now, running late despite having had nothing else to do and nowhere else to be, her heart thudded painfully. The pretence was becoming too much of an impossible act to maintain. She was living as two separate people: the woman she wanted to be, and the one she needed to be. She had thought herself resilient, made of strong enough steel to prolong the performance, but it was proving far more exhausting than she had anticipated – and worse, far more dangerous.

She parked in a pay-and-display car park, paid for a ticket and then headed across the road into the park. There were few cameras, and the ones that were there could be easily avoided. Were they to be seen together by a passer-by, they would look no different to anyone else: mother and daughter taking a stroll; two colleagues sharing a walk during their break.

The playground was busy, many of the children still in uniform, having gone to the park straight from school. It was a sunny afternoon, and the queue at the ice cream van snaked past the playground's entrance. Once Jackie had passed the fenced-off area, the park became quieter. The wide path led to a smaller stretch of walkway that wound beneath overhanging trees. It felt more private here, as though she was momentarily cut off from the rest of the place. She might not have been in London at all, transported to the kind of tranquillity that she had once found in Purton all those years ago.

And then she saw her. She was sitting on a bench near the rose garden, head lowered as she scrolled her mobile phone. Her hair was caught by a stream of sunlight, and for a moment it seemed to spark like flames. She looked up and spotted Jackie, but said nothing as she put her phone in her bag.

Jackie sat down beside her. 'Have you lost your mind? What the hell did you think you were playing at?'

'She's getting away with it and we're letting her.'

Jackie looked away as an elderly couple approached. She waited until they had passed and were far enough away not to hear the conversation. 'We're not,' she hissed, putting a hand on her arm. 'I told you already, you need to play the long game here. You need to listen to me.'

'No,' she said, yanking her arm away. 'Maybe you need to listen to me. You promised me you wouldn't let things go this far. You know what she did. You know everything she's responsible for. Do you ever think of my mother any more, Jackie, or have you forgotten about her completely?'

The words were as cutting as they'd been intended to be. And then there was the name. For as long as Jackie could recall, she had been Auntie Jac. The next best thing to a mother.

'There's not a day goes by when I don't think about her,' she answered quietly.

'Then why are you letting this happen?'

'Did you start that fire?' Jackie asked, already knowing the answer. There was nothing for her to deny when her guilt was unquestionable.

Her face was flushed red; at her sides, her hands had balled into fists. She was her thirteen-year-old self all over again. Angry and bitter. Scared.

'Jesus. The window was bad enough, but this is going too far. You might have killed her.'

'This isn't fair. None of it is fair.'

'I know.'

'She doesn't deserve this life. She doesn't deserve that baby.'

'I know,' Jackie said again, putting her hand back on her arm, as much to silence her as to comfort her. 'But look at me. Look at me,' she urged. The other woman lifted her head, and their eyes met. 'This is not the way. You need to be patient, and you've not got long to wait. If you do anything to harm her now, you'll take away the very thing that will hurt her the most. You understand what I'm saying, don't you?' She spoke the words as she needed them to be understood, solid and resolute.

'I'm sorry,' she sniffled. 'I shouldn't have said what I did. You know I don't mean it. It's just that after everything she did...'

'Don't put yourself through this,' Jackie soothed. 'You're torturing yourself.'

The other woman took a deep breath and exhaled slowly before wiping her eyes. 'How's my make-up?'

Jackie put a hand to her face and gently wiped away a smear of mascara. 'Perfect.'

She smiled and put a hand over Jackie's. 'I don't know what I'd do without you, you know that. I know I've been crap at keeping in touch sometimes, but life has been hard. You've always been the closest thing to a mother I've had.'

'I know,' Jackie said, moving her hand and giving her fingers a gentle squeeze. 'That's why you have to trust me. What if the police find out you started that fire?'

'They won't,' she said, with a confidence Jackie hoped wasn't naïve.

'The only one who's going to suffer is you, and you've suffered enough. Come here.' Jackie closed her arms around Amber and held her close, as she had when she was a child. 'Please be patient,' she told her, pulling away to meet her eye. 'You need to wait for that baby to be born.'

TWENTY-SEVEN

THE MOTHER

'You'll be okay from here?' Callum asked as he pulled up outside Karim's house.

'I'll be fine. And thanks for everything.'

She had expected Karim to live in a sprawling townhouse; instead, he lived in an apartment block in Stoke Newington. The place was nice, and she supposed it offered all the space a single person needed, though she realised she had made assumptions of his lifestyle based on his clothes and his employment.

'What did you think I was doing at the flat that day?' he asked as she followed him into the living room.

'I don't know. With everything that's being going on, I just...' Her sentence trailed to silence.

'Did you think I was involved with that brick?'

'I don't know what I thought.'

He looked hurt, but the truth was that he had shown an unusual interest in her. 'Was that your partner?'

She shook her head. 'Ex.'

She followed him up the stairs to his apartment, and he showed her into the living room. 'I'll put the kettle on.'

While he was in the kitchen, Lauren noticed the photo frames that lined the windowsill. In each there was a little girl, the series of photographs a chronology of her early years: a tiny newborn in an oversized Babygro; a toddler grinning cheekily as she coasted a sofa; a four-year-old posing in her first school uniform. She was a pretty little girl with dark hair and long eyelashes, and Lauren felt a wave of something indecipherable at the thought that he had a family she'd known nothing about.

'My daughter,' he said from the kitchen doorway. 'Zarah.'

'She's beautiful.'

'Thank you.'

Lauren turned to him. 'Why have you been so kind to me? Paying for the window, calling to check everything's okay... It's not normal landlord behaviour.'

'Can't people be kind any more?'

'They're often not.'

Karim gestured to the photographs on the windowsill. 'She would have been fourteen last week.' The past tense echoed between them. 'She died of a brain tumour when she was six.'

'Oh my God. I'm so sorry.' Lauren looked at him, but Karim kept his eyes on the photos. She couldn't comprehend how anyone overcame such a trauma, and if the absent wedding ring was anything to go by, Karim's marriage hadn't been able to survive the tragedy. She remembered the mention of his ex-wife, of her having been in hospital.

'I didn't spend enough time with her,' he continued. 'I was always working. Always making more money. There was always tomorrow or the weekend. Her mother and I meet up every year, on Zarah's birthday. She's just had to have an operation, so that's why I got a bit behind with things.'

'Is she okay?'

Karim nodded. 'I shouldn't be telling you all this. I'm just trying to answer your question. There you have it. I'm simply trying to be a better person.'

Lauren searched for something to say, but there was nothing that didn't sound clichéd. What had happened to his daughter was not his fault, but what comfort was that to him now?

'I'm sorry,' he said, looking at her now. 'Are you okay?'

'Yeah. I'm fine. I'm just... It's heartbreaking.'

He forced a smile. 'Come on, let's get that cup of tea. Do you want something to eat as well? You must be starving.' She followed him into the kitchen, where he set about making tea.

'Did you tell the police about the brick?' he asked.

She nodded. It felt like less of a lie somehow.

'Do you think the two incidents are connected? Why would anyone do this?'

Please stop asking questions, Lauren thought. She suspected the last one was rhetorical, but even so, they all led to places she didn't want to go.

'I've not got much in,' Karim said, closing the fridge. 'Will pasta do?'

'Great. Thanks.'

He handed her a mug of tea, and when she took it from him, she managed to spill some over her hand. It was scalding hot.

'Shit.'

She went to the tap and held her hand under the flow of cold water. She sensed Karim behind her, unmoving.

'What's going on, Lauren? I've had I don't know how many tenants over the years. No one's ever had so much trouble. Bad luck seems to be following you.'

She stood facing the sink, too much of a coward to yet turn to him. He wasn't a fool, and she owed him an explanation. Her suspicion of him had proved the product of an overactive imagi-nation and a lack of organisation, when the truth was he had done nothing but try to help her.

'It's my brother,' she told him. 'I think he might be involved in all of this.' She turned. 'We lost touch for a long time, but I think he's found me.'

'Found you? You make it sound as though you've been hiding from him.'

Lauren took her tea to the table and sat down, awkwardly trying to cover the mess she had made of her sweater sleeve. 'In a way, I suppose I have.'

'Did he do something to you?'

'Not directly. He got himself involved with drugs... they messed him up. He could never keep out of trouble.'

Karim looked at her sympathetically. She didn't deserve it, she thought. 'But you told the police about him?' he asked.

Lauren nodded, but he saw through it.

'I can't imagine how difficult it must be to have to shop a member of your own family to the police. But he tried to kill you. He could have killed your child.' He sipped his drink. 'I'm sorry if I'm talking out of turn. We barely know each other, but you shouldn't be going through all this.'

'Why would you care, though? I don't mean to sound rude, but as you say, we barely know each other.'

'I told you. I'm trying to be a better person.'

Lauren said nothing, but her facial reaction must have spoken more than she'd intended it to.

'You don't think that's believable?' Karim asked. 'More believable than a brick and a fire happening within a month of each other by coincidence, I reckon.'

She felt her face flush. He had known she'd lied to him. Now she was allowing him to think that she was finally telling the whole truth.

'I'm not trying to embarrass you or accuse you of anything. I'm just saying that if you're in some sort of trouble, perhaps I might be able to help you. You need to tell the police about your brother. You're not going to feel safe until you do.'

He got up and went back to the kettle, filling it to boil water for the pasta. 'I have an empty flat in Finchley. I'll take you there after we eat if you like, show you around.'

'Are you sure? You must have things you were supposed to be getting on with today.'

'Nothing that can't wait.'

After they'd eaten, he drove her to the empty property. It wasn't as nice as Lauren's old flat, though anywhere would now feel better than there. Karim waited at the door as she went inside and looked around. She was hardly likely to say no to the offer when she had nowhere else to go.

'You can stay here as long as you need to,' he said, when she returned to the hallway.

'Thank you. I appreciate everything you've done to help me out today. How much is the rent?' She was hoping it would be similar to the other flat. This place was smaller, but she realised it was in a more expensive area.

'Look, I've spoken to my brother and we don't want any rent from you for the first month here. With everything you've been through, you deserve a break.'

'I appreciate the offer, it's really kind of you, but I can't do that. I don't want—'

'It's not charity,' he interjected, anticipating her response. 'It's one person helping another. But there's a condition.'

'What's that?'

'You tell the police about your brother. Today. I don't fancy having another place go up in flames, and I don't want to be getting a call saying you didn't make it out next time.'

Lauren was forced to fight back tears. Karim caught sight of them.

'None of this is your fault, Lauren,' he said.

Oh God, she thought. If only he knew. 'I'd be paying you if I was in the other flat, and I'll be paying you in this one. But as I say, I appreciate the offer, I really do. I'm just grateful to have somewhere to stay.'

'Do you know when you'll be able to get your things?'

'I should get a call this afternoon, I hope. This is only going to be temporary. I'll have to move out of London before my maternity leave finishes anyway. Childcare,' she added, by way of explanation. 'Can we arrange a six-month contract?'

They were interrupted by her phone, which she'd tucked in the waistband of her leggings. She hesitated before answering, wondering whether she would be met once again with nothing but breathing.

'Is that Lauren Coleman?'

'Yes. Who's this?'

'My name's Detective Sergeant Barton, from Thames Valley Police.'

Lauren's heart stuttered. Had they already found out how the fire had been started? Or more... had they found out who was responsible? Then she realised that someone from the local police would be calling her, not a detective from Thames Valley.

'I'm sorry to have to inform you of this, Ms Coleman, but...'

The rest of his words faded behind the rush of thoughts that invaded Lauren's brain. Karim was watching her, his face creased with concern as he witnessed her reaction to a conversation of which he was only audience to half. As the detective finished speaking, Lauren jolted herself back to the present.

Karim eyed her questioningly. 'Everything okay?' he mouthed.

She placed a hand over the phone and lowered it from her face. 'No,' she said quietly. 'It's my brother. He's been found dead.'

TWENTY-EIGHT

THE MIDWIFE

After leaving Amber in the park, Jackie went back to her car. She was shaking by the time she reached it; the lies and the deceit had balled into a mass like a malignant tumour growing inside her. Their plan was a meticulous one, involving months of preparation. It would take one moment, one simple stupid mistake, to bring it crashing around them.

She pressed the back of her skull against the headrest and breathed in deeply through her nose before giving a long exhalation in the way she told mothers to during labour. Trying to concentrate on something other than the pain.

The memory of the conversation came back to her, sharp and vivid. Alive. They had been in the living room, just the two of them. Where had Simon been? She couldn't remember, and it didn't matter. Amber had sat curled into Jackie, her frame so much smaller and vulnerable than her years. They had sat silently like that for some time, Jackie waiting patiently until Amber was ready to speak.

When it had come, the question had caught her off guard.

'What's a guardian angel?'

Jackie had stroked the girl's dark hair, her eyes moving to

the ceiling as she sought the right answer. 'It's an angel who looks after someone, who protects them. You can't see them, but you can feel them there sometimes, when you need them.'

The room was bathed in silence for a moment as the answer was absorbed.

'Like you then. Are you my guardian angel?'

Jackie had smiled sadly. If only that could be true, she'd thought. 'But you can see me, my darling. And you can see me whenever you need me, okay?'

'Okay. Auntie Jackie?'

'Yes.'

'Can I sleep here again tonight?'

'Of course you can.'

After a few months, the spare room at the back of the house had been decorated in a cheery pastel yellow, the bed adorned with a floral duvet, the bookcase lined with a selection of children's titles that they would choose and read together. Simon had been okay with the arrangement – it was only an occasional thing, every now and then at the weekends, and as he was away with work some of the time, it hadn't needed to affect his life too much. Until, of course, it had begun to.

Jackie sighed and turned the key in the ignition. A guardian angel. Someone to look over another and protect them from harm. It was all she had ever striven for, and it was what she would continue to do.

TWENTY-NINE

THE MOTHER

The following days passed in a blur. Lauren had the rest of the week off work, Fiona telling her to take as much time as she needed. She must have realised that Lauren wouldn't make it back before her maternity leave officially started, but she was sensitive enough not to raise the subject. News of Jamie's death had always been expected, a corner of Lauren's brain having prepared herself long ago for the inevitable call, and yet it had still managed to come as a shock. She wasn't sure how she was supposed to feel. She couldn't grieve for him as anyone else might grieve for a brother, not when their relationship had been annihilated years ago. Not after what he'd done. And yet she still felt the loss with a rawness that stung, as though a layer of her skin had been peeled off and the fragile red flesh beneath left exposed to the elements.

Funeral arrangements took up much of her time, though it was the last thing she wanted to have to be dealing with. Even for someone who'd spent two-thirds of their adult life behind bars, the paperwork that arose from Jamie's death was substantial. Although Lauren had always expected that at some point she would be left to deal with her brother's funeral arrangements, she had underestimated the enormity of doing so alone.

She wanted to hate him. She did hate him. She wanted to love him, and despite everything, there was still a part of her that did. He was what their father had made him, the strict rules of their house enforced with such authority that both children had gone on to rebel in their own ways, and yet perhaps their mother had been as much to blame. But above everything else, Jamie was responsible for his part in what had happened, and perhaps that had always been the hardest thing to accept. Regardless of who and what their parents had been, no one had forced him to do what he'd done. Lauren grieved for the life they might have had, the relationship that might have developed had it not been for what had happened that night.

She would never forgive him for what he'd done all those years ago, though it didn't make him responsible for the attacks on her. Now that she knew he had been dead before the fire had been started, she couldn't begin to guess at who might have done it.

She tried to busy herself and keep her mind distracted with making the new flat as homely as possible. She didn't want to exert too much energy, not knowing how long she might be there for, but arranging the furniture and moving in the things that had been salvaged from the old place was a welcome distraction from thoughts of the past. Karim had helped her, collecting her belongings and driving them over. Luckily, all the baby's furniture had survived the fire intact, the worst of the damage confined to the kitchen. The place was still a crime scene while the fire investigation team continued their work, though apart from confirming it had been deliberate, they'd given Lauren no details of how the fire had been started.

After almost a week in which her only venture into the outside world had been to visit the funeral director in Milton Keynes, Lauren needed to go to the supermarket. It was the last thing she felt like doing, but she knew that staying cooped up inside was only going to make things worse. Karim had called, and Fiona too, both with offers to meet with her, but Lauren had made excuses, feigning a busyness she wished was a reality. It wasn't just news of Jamie's death that had kept her indoors. The brick through the window and the shoebox in the garden had been meant to unsettle her, a gentle prelude to the subsequent destruction. The fire was the real warning, intended to rip her world from beneath her. Or worse. Fear had stamped its mark upon her, tattooed now on her skin. Someone had been watching her, someone had been following her; someone had targeted her. The worst of it was that she had no clue who it could be. Everyone was dead, weren't they?

Whoever the person was, she couldn't let them find out where she was, though she knew there was little chance of keeping herself hidden for ever. They had managed to find her before, miles from what had once been home. Tracking her down in the same city would presumably prove a comparatively easy task. Thoughts of who the perpetrator was continued to taunt her. It might have been better for her if the person responsible for tormenting her *had* been Jamie. Better the devil she knew. Now, with her brother gone, the threat of the unknown became even more sinister.

Building herself up to going out had proved to be an effort, and once at the supermarket, Lauren realised she should have made a list. Her trolley contained a mishmash of items, none of which could be put together to make anything that would vaguely resemble a meal. She didn't want to eat. She *had* to eat. Washing powder, she thought, her mind jumping from one product to the next. She'd run out of washing powder.

She stood in the cleaning aisle and looked at the array of detergents on display: bio, non-bio, fragranced, un-fragranced. Her brain couldn't process the choice. She just wanted washing powder. Why had everything in life become so complicated?

'Lauren?'

She jolted at her name before registering recognition. The voice was the midwife's. She turned to find Jackie beside her, basket in hand.

'Everything okay?' she asked. 'We missed you at the mums' group this week. You're feeling all right, are you?'

The group. In the aftermath of the fire, she had forgotten all about it. She should have messaged Jackie to let her know she wasn't going to make it. Much to her embarrassment, her eyes filled with tears. Jackie's was the first friendly face she had seen in days, and just the sight of someone familiar, someone kind, brought with it a rush of relief.

'Oh God, Lauren. What's happened?'

She wiped her eyes with her fingertips as she tried to hold back further tears. 'I'm sorry. You've caught me on a bad day.' She waved a hand casually, as though the moment might be blown away. 'Hormones,' she said with a forced laugh.

Jackie put a hand on her arm and pulled her gently aside, out of the way of passing shoppers. 'Let's get you out of here. Do you want to go somewhere quiet for a coffee and a chat?'

Jackie abandoned the little shopping she had in her basket, telling Lauren she could come back to do it later. Lauren allowed her to take control of the trolley she'd been pushing, and she watched absently as Jackie loaded everything onto the conveyor belt.

'Just as well I'm here,' Jackie said, once Lauren had paid for the shopping. She grabbed two of the bags, allowing Lauren to take the lightest of the three. 'How were you going to get all this home? You don't have a car, do you?'

Lauren muttered a thank you, but it was only as they walked through the car park that she wondered how Jackie knew she didn't have a car. She couldn't remember ever having mentioned the fact. Had she talked about using public transport to get to the community centre? Maybe it was a general assumption that the majority of people who lived in London didn't own a car, even those who lived in the outer areas.

'You're white as a sheet,' Jackie said as they turned down the next street. 'Have you eaten anything this morning?'

Lauren nodded. She hadn't – there had been barely anything in the flat – and she couldn't face even the thought of food. An awful rolling nausea had taken hold of her stomach since the night of the fire. She was plagued with the thought that something was going to go wrong. Something always went wrong.

'Here,' Jackie said, gesturing across the street to a coffee shop. They waited for a gap in the traffic before crossing, Jackie steering Lauren by the arm as though she was elderly or incapable. The truth was, she felt removed from the world. She had drifted through the motions of living for the past few days, a defence mechanism of mental separation that would keep her from falling to pieces.

The coffee shop was warmly lit and inviting, and when Jackie pushed open the door, they were greeted by the smell of cinnamon and vanilla. She held the door open for Lauren and waited for her to go inside. Jackie chose a table near the window, as far from the serving counter as they could get. She watched as Lauren removed her coat and hung it on the back of the chair. 'Tell me what's happened.'

'Ask me what hasn't. It'll be quicker.' Lauren sat down and scanned the menu, though she had no intention of ordering anything more than a cup of tea. 'Sorry. I don't mean to sound flippant.'

They were approached by a girl who looked no older than twenty, who asked if they were ready to order. Jackie ordered a cappuccino and Lauren asked for a decaf tea.

Jackie waited until the girl had gone to get their order. 'What is it?'

Lauren returned the menu to the stand in the middle of the table. 'I got some bad news a few days ago. My brother died.'

Jackie's eyes widened, but there was something else in her expression. She looked surprised by the revelation, as though Lauren's response hadn't been what she was expecting. 'Oh God. I'm so sorry. That's awful.'

'We weren't that close. He... he lived away.'

Jackie was watching her intently. For a moment, Lauren felt uncomfortable beneath her gaze, as though Jackie could somehow see straight through her and was aware of all the things that weren't being said. Then the young woman came back with their drinks, breaking Jackie's focus.

'Had he been unwell?' she asked, once they were alone again. 'I know it's no less of a shock if it's expected.'

Lauren shook her head. 'He had a drug problem. He'd had it for years.'

Would Jackie make a judgement? she wondered. Would her opinion of Lauren change now she knew this about her brother? God only knew what she would make of her if she knew the rest, she thought.

'An overdose? I'm so sorry.'

'He was his own worst enemy in a lot of ways.' Lauren sipped her tea and looked out of the window. When she looked back, Jackie's attention was fixed upon her in a way she found unsettling. Amid the chaos of all that had happened, she had forgotten about the strangeness that had passed between them during their past couple of meetings.

'Do you know when the funeral will be?'

'Next week. I'm grateful there won't be a long wait for it. I'd forgotten how much paperwork is involved in a death, though.'

'If there's anything I can help with...'

'That's kind of you, but I'm mostly finished.' She put a hand to her mouth as she stifled a yawn. 'I'm sorry. I'm so tired all the time. I imagine it's normal at this stage? Anyway,' she added, taking a sip of her tea, 'not long now.'

'No,' Jackie said with a smile. 'Not long at all. Look, if you need anything, any time, you've got my number, okay?' She reached across the table and took Lauren's hand in hers, squeezing her fingers a little harder than was comfortable. 'Don't be on your own.'

THIRTY

THE MIDWIFE

Twenty-three years earlier, Simon had given Jackie an ultimatum. They had been in the garden of the cottage in Purton at the time, the tree that had been planted at the edge of the lawn already as tall as the fence.

'We can't have her stay here any more.'

Jackie had been digging weeds from a flower bed, her knees pressed into the damp soil. She sat back and turned to her husband, who was sitting in a wicker chair reading a newspaper. The late-afternoon sunlight that shone over the garden made his stubble shine silver, though he was yet to hit his mid thirties.

'She needs me, Simon.'

'*I* need you.'

She stuck her fork in the flower bed. Despite her best efforts, the geraniums were wilting. She seemed incapable of keeping anything alive. 'And you've got me. Always. What has that poor girl got? She's just a child. This is the closest thing she has to a stable home.'

'She's not family, Jac. I know that might sound insensitive, but we've got our own family to think of.'

The tree suddenly seemed bigger, as though it was looming over them.

'You need to be looking after yourself. Avoiding stress. And while you're still doing everything for her, you're taking away responsibility from Malcolm. She's his daughter – he needs to start doing his job.'

Jackie didn't think Malcolm was capable any longer of being a father. Grief had ruined him, and in its shadow, addiction had been lurking. He had found a crutch in alcohol, which seemed now to mean more to him than anything else, including his own child. People had tried to help him, but he had rejected every effort.

Behind her, Simon sighed. 'I know you think you're doing the right thing, and I love you for it, you know that. But she can't stay here for ever. It was just the odd night, then it was weekends, now she's here almost every day. I want us to try again, when the time's right. When you're ready. But I don't think you'll ever be ready, not while she's still around. She's too attached to you, Jac. You're not her mother.'

The words stung. She was no one's mother. That was how the rest of the world regarded her, at least. And yet she had been. She was. Though she had carried her baby for only a short time, it had still existed. It had needed her. Now someone else's child needed her.

'You need to talk to her,' Simon said, folding his newspaper and getting up from the chair. 'She needs to go home. It's me or her, Jac. I'm sorry, but that's what it's come to.'

An hour later, she came in through the front door. She no longer knocked, and Jackie had given her a spare key for the days when she was working. She was still in her school uniform, though her bag was nowhere to be seen. Jackie wasn't always sure where she went in the time between school and reaching their house, though she knew she rarely made it to her own home. She had seen her a couple of times in the park, driving there to check up on her, and was suspicious of the company she kept, the other kids older, not from her school. Lynne would have wanted her to keep an eye on her daughter. It was the last thing she could do for her.

'What's for tea?' she asked as she came into the living room. Simon was upstairs in the bedroom. Jackie guessed he had made himself scarce so that she had space to talk to her alone, though she wasn't entirely sure she was grateful for it.

'There's a cottage pie in the oven. But look, there's something we need to discuss.'

She flopped down in a chair and used the remote to turn on the TV. 'What's that?' *Neighbours* was on. A couple were having an argument over an affair the husband had been caught having with his secretary. She turned the volume up.

'It's about... this,' Jackie said, unable to find the right words. 'This... situation.'

She watched as the girl pulled the scrunchie from her ponytail and flicked her hair like a dog shaking itself from the sea. The female character on the soap opera reached for a plate and threw it at her husband, who ducked just before it smashed against the wall behind him.

'Can you turn that down?'

When she didn't respond, still staring wide-eyed but unseeing at the drama unfolding on the screen, Jackie reached to the arm of the chair, picked up the remote and turned the television off. The girl turned to her as though she'd just been scalded. 'I was watching that.'

'We can't go on like this,' Jackie said, hating herself with every word. 'You know I love you, don't you? I know we're not related, but you've always been like a niece to me, and I've always tried to do what I've thought was best for you.'

Her lower lip was sucked beneath her teeth as she waited for Jackie to continue. 'But?' she said flatly.

'But nothing. I'm still doing what I think is best. You need to go home. You and your dad need to sort things out. You're family. You need each other. I've spoken to him this afternoon. He wants you back. He misses you.'

'Right,' she drawled. 'He's missed me so much. Must be why he's been round here every five minutes trying to get me to go home.'

'He has been here,' Jackie reminded her. 'You know that. But we agreed he should stop for a while because he wanted to give you space. We explained that. He thought that if you had a bit of time to think about things, you'd come around to the idea. You've got to go back at some point.'

She moved to the edge of the chair. 'Why? You've never said that before. When have you ever said I'd have to go back?'

'Oh darling.' Was this true? Jackie thought. She couldn't remember. She had assumed she'd realised that her staying with them was only ever meant to be a temporary thing, but perhaps the longer she'd been there, the more she had come to assume it was permanent. Jackie should have corrected that, but how could she have done so without upsetting her or making her feel that she was being rejected?

'You're kicking me out, then?'

'That's not what's happening at all.'

'So I can stay?'

'Look, I—'

'You *are* kicking me out!' She got up from the chair. Her eyes were wet with angry tears. 'Thanks a lot. Thanks a lot for everything. I mean, it's been really nice while it lasted, but I suppose it gets a bit boring after a while. Who wants the kid with all the baggage? Let someone else deal with her.'

When she went into the hallway and headed upstairs, Jackie followed. She had gone into her bedroom and was pulling clothes from the wardrobe. At the sight of them piling up on the carpet, Jackie realised things had gone further than she'd realised. She had been living there. This had become her home. She was right, then: Jackie was kicking her out.

'Look, you don't need to—'

'Shut up,' she snapped. 'You don't want me here, so there's nothing more to say.'

A moment later, Simon appeared in the bedroom doorway. 'Don't ever speak to Jackie like that again, do you hear me?'

'Don't worry. I won't be speaking to her in any way again.'

Within moments, she had gathered her things and fled downstairs. Jackie followed. 'Let me drive you home.'

'I don't want anything from you! You know, nature knows what it's doing sometimes, doesn't it? It was right you lost that baby. You're not cut out to be a mother.'

The following day, Jackie boxed the remainder of her things and took them over to Malcolm's house. He had lost more weight, his cheeks grey and hollowed. He thanked her for taking such good care of his daughter, but there was a silence after the sentence that suggested the words meant something more. Later, Jackie wondered whether there was an indication that he'd wanted that care to continue for longer. When they'd spoken on the phone, he'd said he missed her, that he wanted her home, but perhaps he'd been saying that because it was what was expected of him.

She'd been wrong about one thing. She did speak to Jackie again – sometimes by letter, occasionally via text – but things between them were never the same, their relationship strained by Jackie's supposed rejection. Over the years, they exchanged birthday cards and emails, and whenever Jackie was able to offer help in any way – be it in the form of money or advice – she would accept graciously, the subject of her return to Malcolm all those years earlier shoved under the rug like a stain neither of them wanted to acknowledge. There was a period of non-communication between them later, one that lasted years, but when Jackie got the call from her asking for her help, she had known there could only be one answer.

THIRTY-ONE
THE MOTHER

A little over a week later, Lauren watched a blur of trees and houses pass by as Karim drove them away from London and towards Milton Keynes. She had no idea what to expect when they arrived at the crematorium, having no idea who, if anyone, might show up for the send-off of a man who had alienated everyone he had ever come into contact with. Arranging a funeral hadn't been on her things-to-do-while-pregnant list, and she was grateful that the funeral directors had made things as straightforward for her as they possibly could be. She knew that Jamie's final send-off would be a brief and sparsely attended occasion. Their father had died ten years earlier, and since their mother's death, Lauren had heard nothing from any of the extended family. Ties had been cut years earlier, and with every move she'd made, she had vowed to keep the distance permanent. Nothing good ever came of moving backwards.

When Karim had offered to go with her so that she didn't have to face the funeral alone, Lauren had at first refused. She'd told him both her parents were dead, but beyond that, she had kept her past to herself, as she intended it to remain. She'd hoped that Jamie's probation officer wouldn't show up, so she'd called him to ask whether he planned to attend. Her relief might have been too audible when he'd said he couldn't make it – he was sorry, but there was just too much on at work, and he wouldn't be able to get the time off. Having to explain to Karim why her brother had gone to prison was something she didn't want to have to face, least of all on the day of Jamie's funeral. She could only get away for so long with using drugs offences to explain his multiple sentences.

With few of her formal work outfits now fitting her, and with no maternity dresses suitable for a funeral, she wore black leggings and a long black oversized shirt she'd bought from the supermarket. She was lucky that most of her clothing had survived the fire; she had lost only what had been in the kitchen at the time, the pile of items that had been due a wash and had been left on the floor by the washing machine. When Karim pulled up outside the crematorium, she felt a wave of sickness surge over her.

'Are you okay?' His dark eyes studied her with concern. Lauren flipped open the lid of her water bottle and took a sip. It was the only thing that seemed to keep the nausea at bay.

'You don't have to come in. It won't be a long service.'

'If you don't want me there, I'll wait here. It's up to you.'

He was nicer than she deserved, Lauren thought, particularly following her suspicions of him. A swell of sadness tangled in her gut. She thought of Zarah, the little girl she had seen in the photographs lined up on Karim's windowsill. Though she was grateful that he was there for her, it was too much to expect him to sit through something that would only bring painful memories to the surface.

'You can call me if you change your mind,' he said, removing the pressure on her to find the right answer.

Lauren got out of the car and smoothed the front of her shirt. There was no one outside the crematorium; the hearse was yet to arrive. The funeral director had asked her whether she'd wanted to travel in a car behind it, but it was too much expense and seemed a hypocritical gesture in light of everything her relationship with Jamie had been.

She went to the building and waited just inside the doorway, where she would be able to see the hearse arrive while keeping out of sight of Karim. She felt awkward and self-conscious, regretting her decision now to let him drive her there. He knew that Jamie had been a drug addict and that he'd died of an overdose, but he didn't know the rest of their past. He might have searched for details of her brother online – he could have searched for her name, too – but he would have looked for Jamie Coleman, finding nothing that related to the man Lauren was about to say a final goodbye to. She was uncomfortable with how far she was having to mislead him.

The hearse pulled up slowly outside the building, and the funeral director Lauren had met the previous week stepped out to greet her. There were no relatives or friends among the pall-bearers, the task of carrying Jamie's coffin into the crematorium assigned to strangers, a sad conclusion to a life that had in so many ways been ended years earlier.

Lauren went into the building and entered an almost empty room. The sum of a person's existence, she thought. She was unfamiliar with the few people sitting there. There might have been ex-cellmates; there could have been colleagues from any of the vast number of fleeting jobs Jamie had passed through before his last stint in prison. She noticed that the man from the pizza place hadn't bothered to show up. Jamie had no doubt been replaced already, everyone expendable; everyone quickly forgotten. She turned to face the funeral director, who was now at the front of the room. The ceremony would be brief: no speeches from loved ones, no songs that brought back memories, no montage of photographs accompanied by the soundtrack of a favourite piece of music.

There was a photograph of Jamie propped on a table in

front of the coffin. Should anyone have walked into the wrong room at the crematorium that day, they might have thought themselves an intruder at the funeral of a teenage boy, if the fresh-faced fourteen-year-old grinning from the confines of the frame was anything to go by. Despite the funeral director's initial reluctance, this was the photograph Lauren had chosen. Jamie was properly alive in it, because it had been taken just before he had died for the first time, his young life over not long after it was taken.

'We gather here today to celebrate the life of Jamie Mansfield,' the man began. Lauren flinched, and she felt the baby kick, as though it too was aware of the irony. 'Celebrate' seemed an entirely inappropriate word. The funeral director knew what he'd been and who he was, but Lauren supposed it wasn't his job to make judgements. Everyone's slate was wiped clean after death, so it seemed.

She turned as a prickling sensation crept up the back of her neck. She had experienced it often recently, this feeling of being watched. A man was sitting in the back row. He hadn't been there when the service had started, and when she looked at him, he made a point of avoiding eye contact, his dark gaze kept focused on the front of the room. On Jamie's photograph. Yet he must have realised she was looking at him when there were so few people in the room. She turned back.

A couple of minutes later, the coffin disappeared behind the curtain. Lauren stood, but when she glanced back, the man was already gone.

She grabbed her bag and hurried to the door, hoping to catch him before he left the crematorium grounds. Outside, a group of mourners had arrived for the next funeral. Lauren searched among them, trying to spot the man from the ceremony, but she couldn't see him. She headed out to the main road, desperate to be away from the building. Then she saw the car. It was parked opposite the crematorium gates, the perfect position to watch everyone who came and went. A black Ford Kuga. The same car she had seen outside the flat in Palmers Green. The driver was already behind the wheel. She started to run.

'Lauren!' she heard Karim call.

Unable to find a gap in the traffic, she stood at the edge of the pavement and watched as her stalker pulled out from his parking space and drove away.

Was this him? she thought. Was this the man responsible for tormenting her?

'Lauren.' Karim reached her side and put a hand on her arm. 'What's wrong? What's happened?'

'I thought it was someone else,' she lied.

She felt his gaze burn the side of her face. He didn't believe her.

THIRTY-TWO

THE MIDWIFE

That evening, Jackie finished her shift at 7 p.m. She went home, had a shower, and put on a pair of pyjamas. With her hair still wet, she sat at the end of the bed and sent a text message to Lauren.

I hope everything went as well as it could today. Please make sure you take care of yourself.

She had thought of Lauren throughout the day, wondering how the funeral might have gone. She doubted it was much of an occasion. Who would want to attend the funeral of a man like Jamie Mansfield? The chances were that Lauren hadn't wanted to go. Regardless, she had been there, and it couldn't have been an easy day for her. Too many memories brought to the surface. Too much risk that someone might have used her brother's death to find her there.

Jackie got up and went to the wardrobe. Beside the shoes placed in rows there was a pile of old photograph albums. She took the second from the bottom: a cream and silver pattern with a plastic protective cover. There had been three moves

since she had last looked through it, and its pages were starting
to yellow at the edges. For a long time, revisiting the memories
had been too painful. She ran a finger across Simon's face as she
turned to their honeymoon in the Lake District. They hadn't
had much money when they'd got married, so after an informal
ceremony at the local registry office, they had spent a week at a
B and B in Windermere, from which they'd explored the
surrounding lakes and mountains. She remembered that afternoon vividly. She'd prepared a makeshift picnic – cheese rolls,
dry without butter, pastries she had bought from the local
grocer a few streets away, and a bottle of wine. They'd stopped
midway along the edge of Wastwater to sit and take in the
incredible views across the lake, which had appeared almost too
perfect beneath the radiant sunshine of what had been a beautiful late summer.

In the photograph, the open wine bottle rested between
Simon's knees, and his face was tilted towards the sun, eyes
squinted to keep out the glare. Jackie's head rested on his shoulder, leaning at such an angle that it appeared to be disembodied
from the rest of her. Their smiles were wide; their happiness
real. The image was grainy and poor-quality, taken on a dispos-
able camera; she remembered how they'd laughed at their
attempt to get them both in the picture, not knowing whether
they'd managed to achieve it. After collecting the packet of
photographs from the chemist's once they were home, they had
looked through them together that evening, finding only one in
which both their heads were fully in shot. They'd had it copied
and put it in a frame that sat on the sideboard in the living room,
the original stuck to the fridge with a magnet before years later
being moved to the album.

The image spoke of a love story, when in fact it told a lie.
The truth was that Jackie had been in love with someone else at
the time, a man she had loved for longer than she had even
known Simon. She had first met Peter Greene when she was a

student nurse in her early twenties, but he was older than she was, married with young children, and she knew that regardless of what she felt towards him, it wasn't meant to be. She could never be responsible for tearing apart a family. She dated other men, but she never felt for any of them the way she did towards him, and it was only when she met Simon that she thought she had found someone she could build a future with.

She looked at the young couple in her hands, fresh-faced and full of optimism. Years later, infertility and heartache would have worn away at the fabric of everything they had worked so hard to become. The arguments escalated; resentment grew. Eventually too many things had been said, things that couldn't be unspoken or swallowed back down and erased from memory.

She turned the page. She knew Lynne was in the album somewhere, but she had forgotten she would make an appearance this early. A familiar lump of sadness stuck in her throat as her friend's smiling face looked back at her. They were in a local pub in the village, just down the road from Jackie's house. They had gone there for dinner and drinks to celebrate Lynne's birthday. A pretty striped summer dress covered the swell of her eight-months-pregnant stomach, and Jackie stood behind her, hands resting on her shoulders, as they beamed happily for Malcolm's camera. They had known each other for little over six months, yet they'd connected like women who'd been friends since childhood.

The thought of Lynne brought tears to Jackie's eyes, even after all this time. She smoothed the image with the pad of her thumb, wishing that she could go back in time and make everything different. She might have saved her, she thought. If only she hadn't been so busy with work. If only she had checked in on her that day, even for just a few minutes. Those minutes might have been enough to save her life.

She remembered the last time she'd seen her, three days

before she'd taken her own life. She'd stopped by the house after work, as she had done every evening that week. The house was quiet, the family dispersed to separate rooms by the tragedy of Nathaniel's death, as though gathering together and being forced to talk to one another would mean having to face the reality of what had happened. Every evening Jackie would go in through the back door and find Lynne sitting at the kitchen table. The place was spotless, not because trauma had triggered a compulsive need to clean but simply because no one seemed to be eating anything – the room's original use was redundant.

That evening, she barely recognised her friend. She had lost so much weight in those past nine days, and she'd aged a decade. The light was gone from her face, everything that she'd been before vanished with the loss of her firstborn.

'Have you eaten something?'

There was no response. Of course she hadn't eaten – nor had she showered or dressed. She was wearing the same pyjamas she'd been wearing three days ago.

'Have you seen him?' Lynne said finally.

'Who?'

'Peter,' she snapped impatiently. 'You know he's involved in the case, don't you?'

Jackie couldn't tell her anything, not without incriminating herself. She wasn't supposed to be involved, and yet she had found herself inadvertently drawn in. She needed the truth, as they all did. 'I don't know anything about it,' she replied, hating herself for lying to her friend.

Lynne looked at her for the first time. She was the shell of the woman she had been little more than a fortnight earlier. Jackie couldn't begin to imagine the pain she must have endured. Nathaniel had been her world.

'You've heard what that girl has said about my boy?' Lynne said. 'It's lies, all of it.'

Everyone knew what had been claimed about Nathaniel

Parker, but Jackie knew more than most. She couldn't tell Lynne that, though, not while the investigation remained ongoing.

She sat next to her at the table. 'The truth will come out,' she said, putting a hand on her arm. 'It always does eventually.'

'Eventually,' Lynne repeated. 'But how long could that be? Meanwhile, everyone thinks my son was some sort of monster. And now he can't even defend himself.'

'But you still can,' Jackie had told her, her eyes filling with tears. 'You have to stay strong for him.'

'What good will that do him now? He's gone.'

In her flat in Oakwood, more than a hundred miles and almost three decades from where the conversation had taken place, Jackie closed the photograph album and pushed it aside. Her face was hot with tears, grief and regret balled like a fist in her stomach. She hated herself for not being there when she'd been needed most, something that even after all these years she'd never been able to forgive herself for.

Lynne's death had been needless, and vengeance had always been the inevitable outcome.

THIRTY-THREE

THE MOTHER

The twinges started early on Thursday morning. Lauren felt the first when she was in the shower, a sudden shooting pain that travelled through her groin and up her abdomen. She got dressed and made herself some breakfast, and while she was drinking a cup of tea, she felt another, sharper this time, more centralised and insistent. This was it, she thought. It was happening. She was a little over two weeks before her due date, but that wasn't unusual. Women went into labour early all the time.

She hadn't yet packed a bag ready for the hospital; she knew she should have done it by now, but in the aftermath of the fire and the subsequent move, and with Jamie's death and funeral to deal with, all her plans had gone awry. She stuffed a nightdress and some toiletries into a bag, along with the couple of sleep-suits she had bought ready for bringing the baby home in. Nappies, she thought, frustrated with herself for being disorganised. She didn't have any nappies. The thought sent a wave of panic through her, and with it came another twinge. She leaned forward and clutched her side. The midwives would have anything she was missing. She just needed to get to the hospital.

The thought of being in labour on public transport filled her with horror, but a taxi would cost a small fortune, and she might get to the hospital to find that labour hadn't even yet started. As she made her way to the station, she found that the more she walked, the less she felt aware of the pain. It was no longer enough to describe as a pain even, more uncomfortable than anything else. The bus was unusually quiet, with just one other passenger. She stood near the front despite all the available seating, worried that if she sat down, she might not be able to get herself back up. By the time she reached the nearest stop to the hospital, she felt exhausted, and she flagged a taxi to take her the rest of the way.

The ward was busy, and there were two members of staff at the reception desk. Lauren explained that she thought her contractions had started and was asked to take a seat in the waiting room. When she sat down, she became aware once again of the twinges that pulled low in her abdomen. She winced as a stabbing pain shot through her womb, and her gasp caught the attention of a passing midwife, who called her through to wait in one of the scanning rooms.

'Have a lie-down there,' she said, gesturing to the bed. 'Has anyone seen to you yet?'

'Not yet. Is Jackie Franklin on shift today?'

'Yes, she's in. Is she your midwife?'

'Yes.'

'I think she might have her hands full with a delivery at the moment, but I'll check for you,' the woman said. She took Lauren's notes from her and scanned them before putting them on the desk and leaving.

Lauren waited so long she started to think she had been forgotten. Along the corridor, a woman's cries could be heard, the sound animalistic and harrowing. She felt herself grow hot and sticky, though the room was cool and the window was open. She wasn't ready for this. She couldn't go through it alone. She wished someone was there with her. She closed her eyes and fought against images she didn't want to linger on: blood, after-birth. Silence.

As though the rest of the ward somehow knew what she'd been thinking, the sounds beyond the room stopped. There was something unnerving about the silence, and Lauren almost found herself wishing that the screaming would resume.

When the door opened, the midwife who had seen her earlier returned, with Jackie following closely behind.

'Lauren's been having some twinges,' the first woman explained. 'Thinks they might be contractions.'

'They seem to have eased up a bit in the last half an hour,' Lauren said, her voice filled with apology for reasons she wasn't sure of.

'Let's take a look at you, shall we?' Jackie said. She turned to her colleague. 'I'm happy to take over from here if you want to go back to the birthing suite.'

'Are you sure? Give me a shout if you need anything.'

After the other woman had left, Jackie looked at Lauren with an expression of concern. 'I'm worried about the pressure you're under. You've been through so much recently. The fire at the flat and your brother's death. You must be finding this hard to deal with alone.'

Lauren flinched at her words. She couldn't recall telling Jackie about the fire. The baby gave her a sharp kick to the ribs, and the pain momentarily distracted her. 'I'm not completely alone,' she replied, aware of the defensive edge to her tone. There was Karim, she thought. In some other life, at some other time, she might have wanted to have Karim by her side, someone reliable and permanent. But she had a baby on the way and things would never work between them as they were now. He was looking for a chance to make amends, and she and her child weren't an opportunity for self-improvement. She was going to have to find a way to ease their friendship before it developed into something that would force her to make promises she'd be unable to keep.

'Let's take a look at you,' Jackie said again. 'Try to relax if you can.'

Lauren raised her top, and Jackie put her hands to her stomach. She flinched beneath the midwife's touch.

'Sorry, my hands are a bit cold.'

She turned her head to the side and focused on the wall, made suddenly awkward by Jackie's closeness. Her body tightened as Jackie's fingers pressed into her abdomen, moving around her uterus as she assessed the baby's position.

'Try to relax,' she said again.

It was far easier for her to say than it was for Lauren to do. What she'd thought were contractions had now eased, and she felt foolish for having rushed here. She was left with a headache and slight nausea; perhaps the onset of a sickness bug, she thought – the last thing she needed.

'The baby's head is engaged,' Jackie said. She smiled reassuringly. 'That's a good thing. It's the right time for it.'

She reached behind her and took a Sonicaid from the desk, moving it over Lauren's stomach to find the baby's heartbeat. She tilted her head as she monitored its regularity. 'All sounding perfect.' She lifted the device away. 'I don't think you're in labour yet,' she said, 'although the baby is certainly getting itself geared up for it. More than likely Braxton Hicks. Your body's preparing you.' She put a hand on her arm and smiled reassuringly. 'Everything's going to be fine.'

There was something behind her eyes, something that lay beyond her words. She studied Lauren with a look that carried too much pity. She knows, Lauren thought. Somehow, she knows.

'You're okay to go home for now,' Jackie said as she ripped a length of tissue from a roll and handed it to Lauren to wipe away the gel from her stomach. 'You can call in whenever you want if you think things are progressing, okay? There's always someone here.' She looked up at the door as though checking no one was near to overhear their conversation. 'And you've got my number. You can call me any time of day or night. That's what I'm here for. Now, where are those notes?'

When Jackie turned to the desk to fill in the relevant section of Lauren's pregnancy records, Lauren felt a chill snake through her. She pulled her maternity top over her bump and pushed herself up awkwardly, feeling a need to get out into the fresh air despite the cold that rippled through her. Jackie was kind and generous, but there was something over the top about the effort she was going to. Lauren had no previous experience of midwives or what their role involved, but she felt sure that this level of attention wasn't usual. Did she do the same for all the patients under her care? Lauren wondered. She doubted it.

'You know, don't you?' she said, when Jackie turned to face her. It felt like a stand-off, the two of them armed with secrets, both apparently skilled at building a presence upon lies.

'Know what, Lauren?'

She had been foolish to think she could keep it hidden. Any trained midwife would be able to spot the signs, and someone with as much experience as Jackie wouldn't have had to look far.

'Don't,' she said. 'Please don't do this any more. You already know this isn't my first baby.'

THIRTY-FOUR

THE MIDWIFE

Lauren left hurriedly after telling Jackie she didn't need to maintain her pretence any longer. Jackie easily persuaded her that she was experienced enough to have recognised the telltale signs of previous pregnancy and delivery, and Lauren was able to rely on patient confidentiality, telling her simply that she didn't wish to discuss it any further. Jackie wondered whether she would ever confide in her with what had truly happened. At some point in the not-too-distant future, it seemed likely that circumstances might force the truth from her.

Later that shift, Jackie helped deliver a baby that was eight weeks premature. The little boy weighed just 3 lb 2 oz, a tiny fragile doll in her hands. The days were so busy and the ward such a hectic, stress-filled environment that it was sometimes easy to forget the enormity of her job and the burden of responsibility that accompanied it. In the moments when she was bogged down with paperwork and protocol, the role was much like a thousand others. But the administrative duties were a necessary inconvenience that kept her away from the hands-on act of being a midwife that she so loved, and it was here in the delivery room that she understood the trust that had been placed in her by so many expectant parents down the years. The little life she held in her hands was the most precious thing in the world, and she felt honoured to have played a role in bringing the child into the world. But he was far from safe yet.

For this child's family, the next few weeks would bring sleeplessness and anxiety, a flood of fear that neither parent would likely have expected to face so soon after the birth of their son. Instead of afternoons spent nuzzled against his mother's chest, the little boy would spend his first weeks in an incubator in the neonatal intensive care unit while his underdeveloped organs were given a chance to strengthen. Physical contact would be confined to his tiny fingers locked around his parents', and he would rely on the sound of their voices to continue to develop the bond that had already begun to grow while he was in the womb.

Jackie's heart flooded with a mix of relief and sympathy. Things might have ended so differently in the delivery room; she'd seen it happen on too many occasions. The grief that gripped a room upon the arrival of a stillborn baby was always harrowing, and once her shift ended, she would find it impossible to switch off from what she'd seen. On every such occasion, she would have given anything to remove the terrible pain of people who had been promised so much and left with heartbreak.

That day, she found herself unable to forget the doll-like child she had seen less than an hour ago, isolated within a plastic box, his tiny eyes struggling to open as he tried to acquaint himself with his new environment. She wondered what a newborn felt as it was expelled from the only home it had ever known, pulled from a place of comfort and security into a world that was bright and vast and unknown. Perhaps it was a blessing that no one ever remembered what those first few moments, hours and days felt like.

When she left the hospital, she headed to the staff car park.

She hated driving in London, but her job was such that she needed to be on call, to be available for home visits and appointments at GP surgeries as well as at the hospital. Having transport at hand had also meant she was never far away from Lauren. As she reached the car, she saw Amber sitting on a low wall that ran behind the row of cars. She was wearing a mid-length floral summer dress with chunky black boots, her stick-like calves flashing pale.

'What are you doing here?'

Amber gestured theatrically to her bump. 'I'm pregnant, aren't I? This is a hospital.'

Jackie put a hand on her arm and led Amber across the car park, hoping to get them out of view of the building's CCTV cameras. She didn't want to be seen with her anywhere, least of all in the place where she worked. She might have been the reason she'd been transferred there, but she didn't want their relationship made public knowledge. Yet she knew it was a futile hope to imagine that she might be able to keep it concealed.

'You need to leave.'

'What's the matter, Auntie Jac? Worried that someone might see us together? Why would that be?'

She knows, Jackie thought.

'I hear you got yourself into a bit of trouble at work.' Amber shook her head slowly. 'Not like you to make sloppy errors, is it?'

'How do you know about that?' Jackie tried to keep the tremor from her voice, but it was audible to them both.

'I know everything.' Amber stood and smoothed down the front of her dress. 'We're still going ahead with what we agreed?'

'Of course.'

'So where is she now? Has she gone into labour?'

Amber had seen Lauren here at the hospital. Either she had somehow followed her, or she had already been here when

Lauren arrived. But why would she be? Jackie wondered. Unless she was there to keep an eye on Jackie herself.

'Braxton Hicks,' she said.

Amber made no comment; just stared at her beneath furrowed eyebrows. 'You look tired,' she said eventually. 'You should try to get an early night.' She gave an ambiguous smile before turning to saunter across the car park, making her way to the main road.

Jackie watched her leave, wondering how she had managed to get everything so wrong. There had been signs there, years ago, but she had never wanted to acknowledge them. Regardless of how the girl might have behaved, there was always a reason for it. It was grief, it was anger, it was confusion, it was adolescence, it was trauma. She was never to blame. The poor child had gone through more in a decade than some people endured during a lifetime. Perhaps Jackie's own guilt had blinded her to what Lynne's daughter really was. While trying to do the right thing by her friend, she had failed when she'd been most needed. She had closed herself off from the suggestion that the girl was anything but a victim.

Now the truth was inescapable. Peter had been right all along: Melissa was everything he'd claimed she was.

THIRTY-FIVE

THE MOTHER

1995

There was a cream bathmat. Or it might have been cream once, but time and the trudge of bare feet not yet bathed had turned it biscuit beige. A chipped avocado bathtub with a bottle of shampoo – cheap, supermarket own-brand, apple scented – at the tap end. The window above the sink was frosted, the sky beyond it muted and opaque. It was early evening, daylight already sneaking behind the roofs of the houses. She had come upstairs with stomach pain, thinking she might be sick, but within a short time the cramps had developed from something uncomfortable into something that was threatening to immobilise her.

She gripped the sink and tried to catch her breath, but she couldn't get enough air into her lungs. What the hell was happening to her? That afternoon she had played in a hockey match against another local comprehensive; her team had scored five goals and she had been responsible for three of them.

She had been a little more out of breath than usual, but nothing that had caused her any concern. Now, she could barely stand.

There was a sudden, floor-shaking scream. Her body shuddered with the force of the sound, one too violent to have possibly come from her. But this wasn't her, it couldn't be. This couldn't be happening to her. God, she was dying. The pain was inside her, beneath her, on top of her; it was everywhere and she was a part of it, consumed by its brutality.

She was on the floor. Her mother was there with her. Later, she wouldn't be able to remember when she had appeared or whether she had said anything; all she would recall was her mother frantically pulling towels from the cupboard and clanging things around with an unnecessary amount of noise. Crying. The cross her fingertip formed across her chest before she said a silent prayer.

Then her father. God, her father was there. He would see her like this, he would see what she had done. He would never forgive her.

'Get out!' her mother was shouting. 'Get out!'

She pressed her weight against the door, shutting her father out on the landing. She bolted it, trapping the two of them inside the small, cramped room, and when she turned, she made no eye contact with her daughter, instead setting about her task as though she knew what she was doing. It was only when she came closer, when she crouched at her daughter's raised knees, that the tears in her eyes were visible, the fine sheen of sweat that glistened on her forehead. Her mother was scared, and for a moment, the notion of it was a distraction from the pain.

'You need to push,' she said, her words without emotion, her eyes still not daring to bring themselves to meet her daughter's. 'You need to push now with everything you've got.'

And so she had. She had done exactly as her mother told her, wishing then that she had done everything her parents had ever told her to do and not to do. All the fears they'd instilled in her were nothing compared to this. She was going to die, she kept telling herself. She couldn't do this.

Later, it would begin to feel like a blur, as though she had been drunk. There had been a pain that had pinned her to the floor before a final release of pressure; she had felt the wetness of blood and afterbirth between her thighs, and she knew what had happened, yet she still couldn't bring herself to believe it. She was only fourteen years old. This couldn't be happening to her.

Delirium made her feel strangely weightless, dizziness making the room spin. How could she not have realised?

'Take it! Just take it!'

The room began to return to her, shapes sharpening into focus. She hadn't realised that her father had come into the bathroom. She was still lying on the cold linoleum, which was now a macabre patchwork of smeared blood and afterbirth. All she could hear were her mother's yells, and it seemed strange to her that the room was otherwise silent. She couldn't hear crying. The baby wasn't crying. Wasn't the baby supposed to be crying?

When she tried to speak, no sound escaped her. She tried to sit up, forcing her weight onto her forearm, but she was too weak to hold herself. Her mother had gone somewhere; she was alone. She felt an instinctive urge to see the child she hadn't known she was carrying. She wanted to hold her baby. But there was no baby. When she looked down, she saw the bathmat stained dark and wet, rust-coloured fingerprints smeared into streaks on the floor. She was light-headed and woolly, unable to push herself upright; there was noise on the landing, but the door had been shut so that she couldn't see what was going on.

But she could hear the crying. Her mother's tears.

And then everything fell into a silence that would chill her for years afterwards.

Her mother returned to the bathroom with a clean pair of knickers and a sanitary towel, still avoiding eye contact as she handed them to her. 'Here. You'll need these.' She handed them to her as though her periods had just started and they'd been forced into *the chat*.

'Where's the baby?'

Her mother set about cleaning up the mess as she forced herself up from the floor. She used one of the towels to dab at herself, though the pain was unbearable. When her mother didn't answer her, she asked the question again.

'Not now,' her mother said, and the emptiness of her voice would haunt her for years afterwards.

'Please. What's going on?'

'You tell me,' her mother snapped, making eye contact now for the first time. 'How long have you known about this?'

'I didn't. I didn't know anything.'

Her mother looked at her with contempt, clearly not believing a word. 'How could you not know? Everybody knows, one way or another. I didn't even know you'd...' She couldn't finish her sentence. She looked away again and returned her focus to the lino, scrubbing furiously as though she might somehow undo what had happened.

She knew what her mother was avoiding saying. She didn't even know she'd been with a boy. Neither did she, not properly. She had been naïve for her age, and it was only much later that she had begun to see what had happened that evening differently. They had never spoken about it afterwards. He was in the year above her, so it had been easy to avoid him at school. She should tell him, she thought. He had a right to know.

'Mum. I want to see the baby. Has Dad got it?' It. She didn't even know whether it was a boy or a girl; her mother had told her nothing. 'Please. I'm sorry. Help me. I just want to see my baby.'

The words floated between them, foreign. She'd never so

much as considered that having a child of her own was a possibility. Not now. Not ever, maybe, unless in some future life that was so far away it might as well have existed in another universe. She was still a child herself. She didn't know anything about looking after a baby.

Her mother flung the bloody cloth to the lino. 'I'm sorry, Joanne,' she said. 'It was stillborn.'

THIRTY-SIX
THE MIDWIFE

Six months earlier, Jackie had met Melissa in the Wetherspoons at Victoria station. They had spoken over the phone and messaged each other online in the build-up to the meeting, but this was the first time they had seen each other face to face in over a decade. Jackie had ordered an orange juice and taken it to a table in the far corner of the room, from where she was able to keep watch on the main entrance. Melissa had changed so much in the time since she had last seen her. As a child, she had always had a solid figure, strong legs and a rounded face, and in her younger adulthood her weight had fluctuated with the excesses of a party lifestyle. Now, in her mid thirties, she was waif-like, everything about her thin and sharp-edged.

'Auntie Jac,' she greeted Jackie as she slid onto the bench at the opposite side of the table. She hadn't called her that in over twenty years, any affection between them abandoned the night she had left the cottage in Purton. 'You're looking well.'

Jackie wished she could say the same for Melissa. She looked as though she was battling some sort of eating disorder or drug addiction; maybe both. Lynne's heart would have broken to see her daughter as she was now.

During their phone conversations, Jackie had asked Melissa what she was doing in London. They had talked about the past, about Purton and the lives they had left behind. They had talked about Lynne. Nathaniel. Eventually, after some persuasion from Jackie, Melissa admitted that she had found Joanne Mansfield. Jackie already knew this: it was the reason Peter had made contact with her again after all these years. It was the reason he had encouraged Jackie to meet with Melissa. He was convinced that Melissa was intent on revenge for what had happened all those years earlier. If Joanne's IVF treatment had been successful, a baby would give her the perfect opportunity. Despite everything she had seen over the years, Jackie still didn't want to believe that anyone could be so calculating and cruel. She especially didn't want to believe it of the girl she had once cared for as though she was family.

'We need to talk about what you told me,' she said. 'The IVF. Has it worked?'

Melissa shrugged. 'Not sure yet. Can you believe it? She's got some front, I'll give her that. Look what she did to the first one... What chance has a kid got with her as a mother?'

Opposite her, Jackie pursed her lips. What had happened to Joanne's baby hadn't been her fault, but Melissa was never going to listen to reason. Joanne had already been persecuted once, she and her mother shunned by a village that blamed her for their relatives' actions. They had been forced to leave their home and adopt new identities. The gossip that had swept through Purton and beyond had been laced with venom, the backlash more than the family could ever hope to recover from. The newspapers had run amok with the story, skewing events so that Joanne appeared guilty, but despite everything, she was as innocent as Melissa had been.

'I can help you,' Jackie said.

Melissa's blue eyes trained upon hers. 'What do you mean?'

'I mean I don't want to see you get into trouble. If you do

something impulsive, you might end up in prison. You've already been through enough, Melissa.'

'It's Amber now,' she said with a smile that held no joy. 'Like the traffic lights. Or a weather warning. Be prepared.' She raised her drink to her lips and eyed Jackie over the rim of the glass.

'Let me help you.'

'How? I don't see how you can change anything. If the treatment's worked, there's nothing you can do to stop it, is there?'

'No,' Jackie admitted. 'But I'm a midwife. Patients trust me. I forge relationships with them. If you let me help you, we can work together to make sure she doesn't keep that child.'

'She doesn't deserve to have one,' Melissa hissed.

Jackie reached across the table and took Melissa's hand in hers. 'I know,' she said gently. 'So let me help you.'

Melissa tilted her head back and looked up at the ceiling as she exhaled slowly. When she closed her eyes, Jackie wondered where she went. She felt so sorry for this woman – so much sympathy for the child she had once been, bereft and isolated by trauma. At just nine years old, she had found her own mother hanging from a washing line in the garden of the family home. What sort of mental scarring must that have left? How did any child even begin to move on from something so harrowing?

'Why don't you hate me?' Melissa asked. The question was pitiful, her tone filled with desperate need. She was still that scared child beneath it all.

'I can't hate you. You're the closest thing to a daughter I've got. I loved your mother. I vowed to always look out for you, whatever happened. That's what I'm doing now. I can't let you go through with this on your own.'

'But what I said to you before—'

'You were a child,' Jackie interjected. 'You were angry and

you were scared, and you had every right to be both. It's forgotten.'

The blue eyes studied her, contemplating whether she was telling the truth. This moment was at the crux of everything Peter was asking of her, Jackie realised: if she lost Melissa now, she would never regain her trust. It was a weight greater than she felt able to carry, but this wasn't about her.

'So what do you suggest we do?' Melissa finally spoke.

Jackie glanced around to check no one was listening in on their conversation. 'We wait,' she said. 'Don't hurt her while she's pregnant, that won't achieve enough.' She paused as she remembered Peter's words, a mantra he had drummed into her just the previous day. 'Remember everything she's put you through,' she continued. 'Hold onto it and use it to fuel your patience. If the IVF works, you need to wait until that baby's born. Then you'll have your best chance at true revenge.'

Melissa watched her intently as she spoke. 'How do I know I can trust you?'

Jackie felt a prickling sensation creep through her. She supposed she was going to have to get used to this sensation. She was going to need to equip herself with ways to keep it concealed. 'I'm a midwife. Everyone trusts me.'

THIRTY-SEVEN

THE MOTHER

Lauren lay in bed and tried to escape the nightmare. There was no waking from this one – there never had been – and she lived it over and over, each awful moment and every detail replayed in high definition, as though she was back there in that house, fourteen all over again, bleeding and terrified. Since returning from the hospital, she had experienced intermittent cramps similar to those she'd thought might be the onset of labour. Braxton Hicks, as Jackie had said. A prequel to the real thing. Now she wondered whether anxiety was making things worse, heightening every sensation.

Someone knew where she was and who she was. They knew what she had done. *You can't run for ever.* Was all of this revenge for what had happened that night at her parents' house almost thirty years ago? But who, now, after all this time, might wish so much suffering upon her? Everyone was dead. And it was a lie, all of it – what other people thought had happened was nothing more than a fabrication. But only she knew that.

Less than an hour and a half after her daughter was born, Joanne had buried her at the bottom of the garden. There had been an oak tree there; once, when she was younger, she had built a den around it – a fortress of branches and twigs that she had covered with an old sheet and hidden inside. When she'd emerged shakily into the garden, the earth had been disturbed, a small, shallow grave dug into the soil. Her father must have done it while she and her mother had still been upstairs.

The shoebox was one of hers. Her hockey trainers, the ones she had worn earlier that day. She took a size four. The box looked too small even for the shoes. She couldn't hold her daughter. After begging her mother to let her see the child, she couldn't bring herself to cradle her lifeless body, too terrified by what she had done. She cut a square of blanket. She put the lid on the box. She put the box in the ground. She had done it half blinded with tears and fear, her mother's voice reminding her that no one could ever know what had happened there that evening. They would think she had killed the baby. They would ask why she had never told anyone. She would be taken in for questioning, arrested, interrogated. She would go to prison. With these threats ringing in her ears, she had carried the shoebox to the end of the garden, her feet pressing prints into the rain-soaked lawn. With trembling hands, she had lowered the box into the hole beneath the oak tree.

'We should tell someone,' she said, the words uttered in little more than a whisper, but she was silenced by her mother's hand on her arm. It was a silence that would continue for almost three decades.

She sat up in bed, knowing that sleep would evade her that night. No matter what position she lay in, she just couldn't get comfortable. Her stomach churned with hunger, despite the fact that she had eaten not long before going to bed. She got up and went to the kitchen, where she made tea and toast. The flat was cold, and the unfamiliar surroundings felt oppressive in the darkness. She had always hated these lonely hours, having found out at too young an age the way all the bad things become even more sinister and threatening after midnight.

She ate the toast in the kitchen and returned to bed with her mug of tea. When she closed her eyes, she could see her parents' living room exactly as it had been all those years before: the gas fire, the marble fireplace; the brown-patterned sofa and the green-swirled carpet. She pictured her mother as she had seen her that night, bony and hunched, head bowed. After leaving the garden, she had gone into the house and changed into a nightdress, though she had known she wouldn't sleep that night. Nobody would, the house alive with an awful energy that pumped through the building. She felt weak, too much blood lost; she had been emptied from the head down: thoughts, heart, gut.

'Why didn't you tell us?' her mother asked her, the two of them sitting at either end of the sofa as though this was any other evening. She had already protested that she hadn't known she was pregnant, but her mother still didn't believe her.

'I didn't know,' she sobbed, the words barely audible. 'I swear I didn't know.'

There was dirt beneath her nails, dried mud on her bare knees. Her skin was patched with purple blotches, her pale thighs the colour of raw chicken flesh. There was still blood between her legs, sticky and cold.

'How could you not have known? Nobody can...' Her mother had cut off her own sentence abruptly, unable to speak the words. 'You must have known.'

But she hadn't. She had put on a little weight around her middle over the past couple of months, but nothing that couldn't be explained by the extra food she'd been eating. She had felt fine. Normal. She'd had periods as well; just light bleeds, but light was normal for her, and they didn't always turn up when expected. It had only happened once, but she supposed now that it was all it took.

None of that mattered. All that mattered was the silence, that awful, heart-deadening emptiness that filled the space around them and that she knew even then would stay with her for ever. It felt as though something had been ripped from her, a vital organ removed. She was only a half-person, breathing and speaking but not really there.

'If you'd told us...'

But her mother never finished her sentence. She hadn't needed to.

If you'd told us, things might have been different. If you'd told us, the baby might still be alive.

'You can't tell anyone about this. No one else knows, and it needs to stay that way. You understand?'

She had nodded, but she didn't really understand. Hiding the baby's existence seemed wrong, like branding her as something shameful. She supposed that to her parents that was what the child was. That was what *she* was now.

The same words kept repeating in her head, taunting her with their finality.

I killed her. I killed my baby. I'm a murderer.

'Tell me his name.'

Both she and her mother started at the sound of her father's voice from the living room doorway. His face was dark and stern, eyes narrowed as their focus landed upon her. She felt like prey beneath the scrutiny of a predator, small and vulnerable. Defenceless. He looked possessed somehow, deranged, as though he might be capable of anything. She had always feared his temper, but knew she had never seen it at its full capacity: there had been no reason for it to make an appearance, not when the rest of the family adhered so carefully to his rules, fearful of the consequences of breaking them. She hadn't been thinking about them on the night she must have got pregnant, though. She wasn't at home. For a short while, she'd been free to do as she pleased.

'His name, Joanne. Who is he?'

She shook her head. What difference did knowing his name

make now? It wasn't going to change what had happened. It wasn't going to bring the baby back. She wouldn't do this to him. He would hate her as much as everyone else would. They would all think she'd killed her.

Her, she thought. She hadn't even had a chance to give her baby a name.

'Who is it?' her father pressed, his voice lowered, threatening.

'I know who it is.'

Jamie. Standing in the doorway to the living room, he had been quietly watching the scene unfold, waiting for his moment to wreak chaos upon them.

'I saw them together outside the church hall,' he said, unflinching, refusing to look in his sister's direction. 'I know who he is.'

Lauren was jolted from her waking nightmare of the past by a noise, something distant and muted that sounded like a gunshot. The details of her parents' living room melted away; she was returned to the flat in Finchley. Her body tensed. It was the night of the fire all over again. Whoever had started it had followed her here. When she heard it again, though, she realised it was a car backfiring somewhere in one of the neighbouring streets. She began to relax, grateful to have been torn from the memories of that night.

Then she felt a jolt inside her, like nothing she had felt before. It was as though she had been punched from within, a sudden sensation like a bubble popping deep in her groin, and she had a sudden urge to use the toilet. She got out of bed and left the room, but she hadn't made it as far as the bathroom when her waters broke in a puddle at her socked feet.

THIRTY-EIGHT

THE MIDWIFE

Jackie was woken by her phone on the bedside table. Lauren's name flashed from the screen. She answered it quickly, knowing something was wrong. It was 3.15 a.m. Lauren had never called her on her mobile, despite having had her number for some time.

'Lauren. Is everything okay?'

'Jackie, I'm sorry, I...' She couldn't finish her sentence.

'Take a deep breath. I'm here.' Jackie felt her heart rate start to quicken. Was she having contractions? When she'd checked her over the previous afternoon, there had been no evidence that she was in the early stages of labour. If there had been, she wouldn't have let her out of her sight.

'I can't, my waters have broken.'

She silently timed the gaps between contractions, hearing the surge in pain with the breathlessness of Lauren's voice. They were coming close together. This sometimes happened: there was no pattern with pregnancies. One might take days, with a slow build of labour symptoms, while another could appear spontaneously, offering little in the way of warning.

'Are you at home?' she asked.

'Yes. I mean... I'm at a new flat.'

'Have you called an ambulance?'

'It's not going to get here in time. Oh God!'

Jackie tried to offer reassurances, but she knew they were futile. She understood why Lauren had been so reluctant to consider a home birth. She had delivered a baby at home before; why would she want to go through that again? She needed to be immersed in the security of a medical setting: nurses and pain relief; doctors on call should one be needed.

But maternity units were not always the secure places they might be assumed to be – Jackie knew this all too well. Five years earlier, she had experienced an attempted abduction on the neonatal ward, when the father of one of the newborn babies – a man who'd been given a restraining order after stalking his ex-partner – accessed the ward and tried to smuggle the baby from the hospital in a holdall. Had the man not aroused the suspicions of another patient, who'd alerted a member of the catering staff, he might have managed to escape with the child. It was exactly this that had raised both Peter and Jackie's concerns about Lauren's labour.

'I'm coming over, okay?' she said, pulling on a pair of jeans as she balanced the phone between her shoulder and her ear. She tapped Lauren's new address into her phone as Lauren managed between gasps to recite it. 'I won't be long.'

The drive from her flat to Lauren's could take anything up to half an hour at the busiest time of the day, but in the middle of the night, with little traffic on the roads, she reckoned she could do it in half that. The chances were that she would get there before the ambulance did.

'I can't do this,' Lauren was saying, her words clipped with the onset of a new wave of pain.

'You've done it before. You can do it again. Get some towels and some warm water if you can. I'm on my way.'

In the car, Jackie called Peter. He answered after just a couple of rings. 'Lauren's gone into labour.'

'Where is she?'

'At the new flat. I'm on my way. She admitted to me yesterday that she'd had a baby before. She must have realised she wasn't going to be able to keep it a secret for ever. I'm scared,' Jackie admitted. 'None of this has gone to plan. I saw Melissa yesterday too – she knew Lauren had been at the hospital. She asked me whether her labour had started and I told her no, but I don't think she believed me.'

'You need to stay calm, Jackie. You can do this, okay? I'm on my way.'

He ended the call, leaving Jackie to make her way to Lauren's flat. She was grateful that the roads were so quiet, while dreading what she might face once she arrived. Dreading *who* she might face.

When she got there, Lauren was waiting behind the door. Jackie had a portable monitor that she'd found in the car boot – the only piece of equipment she would have to help her with the delivery.

'Oh, thank God.' Lauren moved aside for Jackie to go in, then lurched forward as another contraction surged through her.

'Come on,' Jackie said, taking her by the arm. 'We need to get you comfortable.'

She had managed to get the things Jackie had mentioned. There was a pile of clean towels at the end of the sofa, and on the floor beside it was a bowl filled with water.

'Can we use this?' Jackie asked, gesturing to the throw on the sofa.

'Whatever,' Lauren said breathlessly. 'Oh shit.' She doubled over as another contraction took hold.

Jackie led her to the middle of the room and made her

comfortable on a makeshift bed put together with cushions and the throw. When she assessed her, it was clear that she was already fully dilated. This baby wasn't going to wait for an ambulance.

THIRTY-NINE

THE MOTHER

The pressure that had built in Lauren's groin felt as though it would tear her in two. Jackie left her on the living room floor as she called 999 to find out how long the ambulance would be. They both knew it was futile. They were going to have to deliver this baby alone.

Lauren cried out as a stabbing pain cut through her right hip.

'The baby's probably pressing on a nerve,' Jackie said. 'When the next wave comes, I need you to push as hard as you can, okay? Whatever's happened before, it's not going to happen again, okay? You are going to be fine, Joanne. The baby is going to be fine. I promise.'

Lauren flinched. No one had called her Joanne since the night her mother had died, and it had been so long since she had heard the name that it sounded alien. But she could never escape who she was – she'd always known that. She could never escape what had happened. The thought that Jackie knew her far better than she had realised was momentarily obliterated by a contraction so strong she thought it might tear through her abdomen.

'How do you know me?' she gasped. 'Who are you?'

She had been right to be cautious of the midwife, she thought. The doubts that had at times crept in had had every right to be there. She'd been right to wonder whether Jackie afforded the same attention to every expectant mother under her care; her suspicions had been justified. Yet now she feared she hadn't been cautious enough. Was Jackie the woman responsible for the campaign of terror that had been inflicted upon her over the past couple of months? When Lauren had been at the hospital the previous day, Jackie had mentioned the fire at the flat. But Lauren had never told her about it, she was certain of that.

'Was it you?' she said, words spoken through gritted teeth as she tried to hold back the pain that threatened to surge again. 'The fire? The brick through the window? The doll?'

Uncertainty flickered behind Jackie's eyes as she absorbed Lauren's flurry of words. 'Doll? What doll?'

Lauren cried out. Regardless of who Jackie was or what she wanted from her, she was the only person now able to help her. She couldn't do this alone. She couldn't lose another baby. 'I need an ambulance,' she gasped. 'Please. I need to get to the hospital.'

Jackie tried to reassure her with a flood of encouraging words. But Lauren could no longer believe any of them. Jackie had been lying to her this whole time, using kindness as a way to get close to her and gain her trust. But why? Who was she? This woman she'd thought had wanted the best for her might be nothing more than a monster. She was back there in that bathroom, fourteen again. The living room floor became a stretch of lino; the midwife's hands became her mother's.

'Who the fuck are you?' she snarled, pain morphing her into a creature she didn't recognise.

'You need to calm down,' Jackie told her firmly. 'I'm here to help you. I've always been here to help you.'

'Then what...'

But Lauren couldn't speak. She felt an intense pressure between her legs. The baby's head was trying to break through, but she didn't have the energy to push. She wasn't strong enough.

'Take a moment now,' Jackie said, as the wave subsided. She moved the monitor across Lauren's stomach as she searched for the baby's heartbeat. 'Deep breaths.'

Lauren tried to force her mother's voice from her mind. *If you'd told us... You can't tell anybody about this.*

The baby's heartbeat sounded through the monitor, strong and regular.

'On the next one, we're going to do it all again, okay?' Jackie said, moving back between Lauren's legs. Lauren felt the other woman's fingernails digging into her right thigh, perhaps a deliberate distraction from the nerve pain that still shot through her groin like a flame.

With the next contraction, she pushed with everything she had. She fought back the demons that raced towards her: the bloodied lino, the shoebox, the lifeless baby. *It wasn't your fault,* a voice told her. *You were just a child.*

'Good,' Jackie said. 'Well done, Lauren, you've got this, okay?'

She reached up and wiped Lauren's forehead with a damp cloth, the gesture so unexpected and strangely intimate that Lauren felt herself overcome with a wave of sadness that momentarily replaced the pain. She had no idea what this woman might do to her. She had no idea what intentions she might have for her baby. Throughout her pregnancy, she had been plagued with doubts, but perhaps danger had been closer than she had ever recognised.

'How did you know about the fire at my flat?' she asked breathlessly.

'Sorry?'

'Yesterday, when I saw you at the hospital. You said something about me being stressed after everything I'd been through. Then you mentioned my brother and the fire. I never told you about the fire.'

'I don't know,' Jackie said. 'You must have mentioned it for me to have known about it.'

'Please stop lying to me. Did you start it?'

A look of horror stamped itself upon Jackie's tired face.

'God, no. I could never do something like that. I—'

She was interrupted by a low groan that seemed to come from deep within Lauren, growing in volume and intensity. Her nails clawed at the laminate flooring as another flood of pain ripped through her. The scream that joined it filled the room, raw and animalistic. As the contraction subsided, the doorbell rang.

'Thank God,' Jackie mumbled as she got up from the floor and went to the front door. Lauren heard a noise, a bang as though the door had been pushed open too hard. Moments later, Jackie returned to the living room, but there was no paramedic with her. The woman standing in the doorway was Amber, and yet she also wasn't. In her skinny jeans and sweater, her stomach was completely flat. There was no pregnancy bump. There was no baby.

She was holding a knife to Jackie's throat, the midwife's eyes wide with fear.

'Don't do this,' Jackie whispered, the words barely audible. 'Please.'

Lauren's eyes darted from one woman to the other. They knew each other, but not in the way she had been led to believe. Not in the way Jackie had told her.

'What are you doing here?' she managed through the pain. 'What the hell is going on?'

Why was Amber there? How had she even known where Lauren lived? She looked desperately at Jackie, whose guilty face offered no answers. Lauren realised she had no idea of their relationship; no idea what intentions either of them really had towards her. She had no clue who the midwife really was. She didn't know who either of these women really were.

FORTY

THE MIDWIFE

'Hi, Lauren,' Melissa said flatly, her expression devoid of the friendliness it had once managed to wear like make-up. 'Or should I call you Joanne? You don't remember me, do you?'

Lauren shook her head. 'Don't do this, please.'

Jackie was acutely aware of the blade at her throat, its tip pressed against her skin as a reminder that she was to do exactly as she was instructed. Where was Peter? He was supposed to be here. This wasn't the way things were meant to happen.

'My name's Melissa Parker. Bet you remember me now, don't you?'

Lauren didn't know Melissa, but the surname gave her the answer she'd been looking for. Nathaniel's little sister.

'I don't blame you for forgetting about me. Everyone else did. You get a lot of attention when you're dead, apparently. How was I supposed to compete with that?'

'Melissa—'

'Shut up.'

Jackie gasped as the knife tip was dug into her spine.

Lauren groaned in agony as the next contraction pushed her to the floor.

'She needs me,' Jackie pleaded. 'I need to get this baby out.'

She felt a shove in the back as Melissa let her go. 'Don't try anything stupid.'

She rushed to Lauren's aid. She could see the crown of the baby's head, but Lauren's energy was fading fast and she was struggling to push any harder. Pain relief would have made this so much easier for her, but she had done this before; now fate had decided she was going to have to do it again. She returned the monitor to Lauren's stomach. The heartbeat was audible instantly, but it was faster than before, erratic, the baby somehow aware of the danger that existed within the new world awaiting its arrival.

'We can't rely on that ambulance getting here in time,' Jackie said to Lauren, trying to ignore Melissa's presence and the knife she still gripped. 'The baby's distressed. We need to do this now.'

Lauren's body shuddered with the next wave of pain that rushed through her. Standing behind Jackie, Melissa smiled wryly, taking a sick pleasure in witnessing the other woman's agony.

'Is it like the first time?' she asked tauntingly. 'You'd think you'd be a bit loosened up, wouldn't you?'

'Melissa, stop.'

'How do you know her?' Lauren managed through the pain.

Jackie felt a sting at the note of betrayal in her voice. Lauren had thought she was a confidante, someone she could trust. Jackie still wanted her to believe those things, though there was little chance of that now. All Lauren would see was a woman who had exposed her to danger; a woman who had brought her worst nightmare to her door.

'She's known me since I was a kid, haven't you, Auntie Jac? She knew my brother as well. She was one of the family.'

The past tense was an intentional attack. Melissa felt as

betrayed as Lauren must do; more so in many ways, because she'd believed Jackie was involved in all this to help her. She had used a slew of emotional blackmail during the past months, reminding Jackie that participating in her warped plan for revenge was the only way to prove she had loved Nathaniel and their mother as much as Melissa had. But Jackie had known for a long time that this wasn't about love. It wasn't even about Nathaniel and Lynne any more. It certainly wasn't about the niece she had never got to meet. Melissa did everything for herself, spurred on by her desire for violence.

Jackie held a cool flannel to Lauren's head as she tried to hush away the pain. She wouldn't rise to Melissa's bait, not while Lauren and the baby needed her.

'You promised me she wouldn't get away with what she did.'

'Push through the pain this time. Now!'

From the corner of her eye, she noticed Melissa's fingers tighten their grip on the knife handle. Jackie's lack of response was exacerbating her rage.

'You were my guardian angel, do you remember that? Everyone left me except you. You were the only constant. I thought you and Simon would rescue me from my life, that we might be a family together, but you never really wanted that, did you? Or was he the one who didn't want it? Either way, it was all lies.'

'Of course I wanted you there. You would never have lived in my house if I hadn't wanted you.'

'So it was him, then?'

Simon had been patient at first, making allowances for the tragedies Melissa had endured in her young life. But his generosity had been stretched beyond capacity, and he had started to resent having her there. On more than a few occasions he had accused Jackie of being blindsided by her, naïve to her manipulation. Perhaps all those years ago, at even so tender an age, Melissa's true nature was visible to Simon where it hadn't been to Jackie. Everyone else had seen her as a vulnerable child. A victim. Everyone other than Peter, who had always claimed she was a monster, and had seen his career jeopardised while trying to prove it.

'Now isn't the time for this,' Jackie hissed.

'Then when? We've never really talked everything through, have we? You just bought your way back into my life with handouts. You sent me back to that house to live with my dad, knowing I didn't want to go there. Knowing that he couldn't cope any more. Do you know what he once said to me? That it should have been me and not them. That I should have died instead.'

Her words cut Jackie, but she refused to let it show. Malcolm Parker had been ruined by the deaths of his boy and then his wife: two losses less than three weeks apart that had torn through everything that had been his life. The last time Jackie had seen him, he had near drunk himself to death. He hadn't coped with caring for Melissa, but his mental absence had been considered a reaction to the tragedies. But what if there had been more to it? What if Melissa had been the root cause of so many of Malcolm's later demons?

'None of what happened is this baby's fault,' Lauren gasped.

'Shut up! I swear I will cut that baby from you, you lying bitch.'

Melissa swung towards Jackie, who grabbed her by the arm. 'Don't do this. Please. Remember what we said.'

'All lies,' Melissa scoffed. 'You didn't mean a word of it.' With the casual ease of someone slicing an apple, she ran the blade along Jackie's bare forearm. Bright blood bubbled to the surface of the wound, and she felt Lauren flinch at the sight of it. Her arm throbbed, but she couldn't panic Lauren. The baby was already distressed, and they were running out of time. She wasn't going to let this happen to her again.

'Look at me,' she said, gritting her teeth through the pain. 'We need the biggest push of all this time, okay? You're almost there.'

She kept her eyes on Lauren's, willing her to keep focus. The more she could distract her from Melissa's presence the better, although after what had just happened, she knew it was hopeless. Lauren scratched at the floor like a wild animal when the next contraction took hold. Fear and necessity seemed to grip her, her body possessed by a primitive instinct that would get this baby home safely. The baby's head was out further now, tiny flecks of dampened dark hair visible on the crown.

'When you get that thing out, you give it to me,' Melissa instructed. She waved the knife, a reminder of what she was capable of if Jackie did anything to disobey her.

'Don't do this,' Jackie said. 'She's suffered enough. She didn't kill Nathaniel. She didn't take your mother's life either. She's had to live all these years with everything that happened, in just the way you have.'

Melissa's face was flushed pink, her eyes wet with tears of anger. 'How can you say that? She might not have beaten Nathaniel and she might not have tied that washing line around my mother's neck, but she's still the reason they're both dead!'

'Oh God.' Another surge of pain ripped through Lauren's body. 'I can't do this,' she said, tears streaming from her face now. 'It's going to kill me.'

'You *can* do it,' Jackie said, leaning forward to place a hand on Lauren's arm. 'Not long now, I promise.' She noticed the blood that ran down her own arm, and tried to blank out the pain that still pulsed through it.

'He never raped you, did he?' Melissa said accusingly.

Lauren shook her head wildly. 'I never said he did. I never told the police he did.'

'Liar.'

'It's true,' Jackie told her. 'It was her parents who said that, not Joanne.'

'How would you know?' Melissa retorted. A look passed between them, and Jackie saw a shadow of realisation fall over the other woman's face. 'How would you *know?*' she repeated.

Jackie moved her focus back to Lauren. There was still no recognition from all those years ago. But then why would she remember her? Their meeting was brief and had taken place amid the most traumatic experience of Joanne's young life. Jackie had been just one more person in a wave of faces that had passed through the room that day.

'I just know,' she said, refusing to admit to Melissa that she'd had any involvement in the case.

'You're a liar,' Melissa spat. 'You're no better than she is. I thought you were on my side.'

Jackie said nothing. If this had ever been about choosing a side, she could never have been on Melissa's. Peter had been right all along: she was dangerous. He was probably right about her part in the death of Becky Hargreaves, and they had no idea what else she might have been responsible for. Revenge had intoxicated her, violence becoming a part of who she was. It was easy to disguise for someone who was able to wear a mask of respectability.

'If you do this now,' Jackie told Melissa, 'you're no better than they are. You're Jamie Mansfield... you're Trevor Mansfield... you're one of them.'

'I don't care. That family took everything from me. She doesn't deserve this baby, not after what she did to the first one. She buried her, for fuck's sake. She put a baby in a shoebox and she put her in a fucking hole in the ground. Why should she get to have a happy ending?'

Jackie tried to push aside the words as she focused on the

baby's head. Lauren was crying now, anguish contorting her face. It wasn't just Melissa's words that were responsible. She knew that her baby was in danger. Her worst fears had taken hold and were growing in strength. If Jackie didn't get this baby out soon, there would be no happy ending.

FORTY-ONE

THE MOTHER

She was never going to get to meet her baby. It was going to kill her first. The pain was everywhere: beneath her, inside her, on top of her, crushing her to the hard floor. Something bad was going to happen, with or without Melissa. She knew it, and Jackie knew it too: it was written all over her face, though she was trying desperately to maintain an illusion of calm. Blood still pumped from the cut Melissa had sliced into her skin; it must have hurt like hell, but Jackie did nothing to show her pain. Instead, she focused on Lauren, offering constant reassurance in the face of the tirade of accusations Melissa continued to throw at her.

Maybe she was wrong. Jackie wasn't trying to hurt her; she was trying to protect her. Yet she had exposed her to Melissa, orchestrating their meeting at the support group. Nothing made sense, but none of it mattered now. All that mattered was the baby. She could do this, she thought. She had done it before; she could do it again. No one was going to take her child away from her this time.

'I am going to take your baby,' Melissa said calmly, as though she had read the fears that must have printed themselves on Lauren's exhausted face. 'You already know that, don't you? If Jackie tries to stop me, I will kill her. If you try to stop me, I will kill you.'

'I need a big push from you on the next one, okay? Keep looking at me, Lauren.'

She was grateful for Jackie's attempts at distraction, but her efforts were impossible. The midwife's hands were shaking with terror. She feared every word Melissa spoke as much as Lauren did. God only knew what this woman was capable of.

'Condolences about your brother, by the way,' Melissa said. 'I don't think he suffered. He was pretty much out of it already by the time I injected him. A shame, really. After what he did to my brother, I should have tortured him.'

Lauren gasped as the truth of what had happened to Jamie hit her. She looked away from Jackie and her eyes met Melissa's, grey as steel and ice cold, eyes that offered nothing back. She had thought he'd died as he had lived most of his life: alone and intoxicated. Now, knowing his death had been by the hand of someone else, she tasted bile as it rose in her throat. An eye for an eye. Nathaniel. Jamie.

Melissa stared back at her, unblinking. There was no remorse, no compassion. She was devoid of feeling, apparently numbed to the terror she inflicted. 'What?' she said, her voice laced with a sinister mock innocence. 'You didn't think I'd let him get away with what he did?'

She stepped towards her, and Lauren felt Jackie flinch against her leg. 'We got stoned together. He thought he'd got lucky, but I was the lucky one. He made it all so easy for me.'

She dropped to her haunches beside Lauren, a look of disgust crossing her face when she looked down between the other woman's legs. 'I only wish he'd suffered more. I wish he'd suffered a fraction of what he put Nathaniel through. You know what they did, don't you? You must have read all about it at the time. Did you read it again? Sixteen separate head injuries.

What chance did a fifteen-year-old kid have against an older teenager and a grown man?'

Melissa wiped away tears with her sleeve. Her eyes were red-rimmed and bloodshot, yet she kept her focus on Lauren, forcing her to consume every word. 'They left him on the ground like a dog. They left him to die alone. It was only fair that Jamie got the same treatment, don't you think?'

'I didn't know,' Lauren said through a sob, knowing that any effort to reason with Melissa would be wasted. 'I didn't even know that Jamie and my father had gone out that night. I never gave them Nathaniel's name.'

'I didn't even know I was pregnant,' Melissa said in a whining tone, cruelly mocking the words Lauren had repeated to her mother all those years ago, words that had been taken and used against her by a local press intent on seeing what remained of her family hounded from the town. 'You didn't know much, did you? Are you really that stupid?'

Lauren couldn't respond, the next rush of pain so intense that she knew this was it: the baby was going to leave her. This was the point at which her child would be vulnerable to the world and everyone in it, their physical separation a reminder of her own limitations. With a cry that felt strong enough to shatter the windows, she pushed every ounce of pressure she could through her hips.

'Again,' Jackie said urgently. 'You're almost there.'

For a moment, Lauren left herself. She saw herself as though floating above her body; she watched as Jackie pulled the slippery, screaming child from between her legs. The moment was fleeting before she was sucked back to the floor, back to her body and the pain that held her prisoner within it. She gritted her teeth and pushed with everything she had, and a last burst of pressure expelled the baby completely from her.

She felt delirious, within herself but also not. And then she heard her baby's cries, sharp and insistent. The sound flooded her with relief, the pain forgotten. Exhausted, she propped herself up on an arm and watched as Jackie turned to Melissa.

'I need to cut the cord,' she told her.

Melissa raised an eyebrow. 'You think I'm going to give you the knife?' She glanced at Lauren dismissively. 'I'll do it.'

'No,' Lauren gasped.

'Okay.' Melissa shrugged. 'She'll have to stay attached then.'

She. Lauren's heart skipped a beat at the news that her child was a daughter. Another little girl. A second chance. 'Please let Jackie cut the cord,' she begged.

'What do you think I'm going to do, quarter you? Now there's an idea.' She raised the knife. They all knew she meant it. She had already admitted to being a killer.

Lauren braced herself for a pain that never came. Instead, Melissa stepped back and wiped the knife on her sleeve with a look of disdain as Jackie lifted the baby and wrapped her in one of the towels Lauren had prepared earlier.

'You need to deliver the placenta now,' Jackie instructed her.

Lauren pushed herself up, wincing at the pain that throbbed through her. She hadn't realised how much blood she had lost until she looked down and saw the laminate flooring decorated in a macabre patchwork of red and brown smears. She probably needed stitches, but she couldn't think about that now.

'Give her to me.'

'Melissa, please—'

'Shut up!' Melissa slashed the knife through the air, narrowly missing Lauren's face. 'Give her to me,' she said again, as Jackie stood and took a step back, the baby held tightly to her chest. Lauren caught the look in Jackie's eye. She was terrified, still clinging to the hope that despite everything she was, Melissa wouldn't be able to bring herself to harm a newborn child.

'Jackie,' she pleaded. 'Stop her. You don't understand—'

'I do,' Jackie cut her short. 'I know everything. I was there.'

'Melissa,' Lauren said, confused by Jackie's admission but desperate to stop Melissa from taking her baby. 'You don't want to do this. No matter what's happened, she's just a baby. She's innocent. If you do this now, there's no going back, you understand that, don't you?'

Melissa's face was hardened, her mouth fixed in a grimace. Her knuckles were white around the knife blade, resolute and unflinching. 'There's already no going back.'

She lunged forward, and for a moment the knife disappeared from Lauren's view. As Melissa and Jackie grappled for the baby, she screamed for them to stop. She pushed herself up from the floor, almost falling over, her body weightless and dizzy. The room swayed around her as the two women struggled, before an awful sound cut through the noise and separated them. Lauren watched in horror as Jackie staggered back, the knife embedded in her side. The baby was already in Melissa's arms.

'Give her to me, please,' Lauren begged.

She wanted to take everything back, all the bad things that had ever happened and that she had been a part of. She wanted to bring back Nathaniel, Jamie, her first baby. This baby. But there was no baby. Melissa and her daughter were already gone.

FORTY-TWO

THE MIDWIFE

In the summer of 1995, Jackie Franklin had been a paediatric nurse working at a hospital in Swindon. As part of her ongoing training, she was requested to assist a police doctor with the medical examination of a minor. It was a particularly sensitive case: a fourteen-year-old girl had given birth to a baby at her parents' house, having apparently had no idea that she was pregnant. Though the girl hadn't been arrested, there was the offence of preventing the lawful burial of a person still to be considered – one that applied to both the girl and her mother.

The girl had been sitting on a plastic chair when Jackie had first seen her. She looked even younger than fourteen, skinny and pale, terror etched into her small features. Jackie followed the doctor into the room. Beside the girl was her mother, equally pale. She barely made eye contact with anyone else in the room, answering questions with as few words as possible. Jackie couldn't imagine the shame she must have felt. Her husband and son had been accused of the most terrible of crimes, and no circumstances were going to justify what they had done.

'Hello, Joanne. I'm Dr Vine.' The doctor reached for a spare plastic chair and pulled it forward before sitting down. She had been chosen specifically for the case based on her gender and her age; she was a mother of two teenage girls, considered by her colleagues someone who inspired trust. 'I understand you've been through a lot in the past couple of days,' she said. 'I was wondering if you could talk me through it. In your own time.'

Joanne didn't speak. No one had been expecting her to, not with so much tragedy hanging over her. The poor girl was probably in a state of shock. It was less than twenty-four hours since she'd given birth. Her brother and father were being held in custody at the same police station, an eyewitness having seen the end of the attack on Nathaniel Parker. Elizabeth Mansfield had said little in response to what her husband and son had done, other than claiming to have had no idea where they had gone when they'd left the house the previous night. Jackie found that difficult to believe, but there was no evidence to prove otherwise. It would be for the police to decide who was guilty, and of what.

'Your mum told us you had no idea you were pregnant?'

Dr Vine looked to Mrs Mansfield, who cast her eyes to the floor and said nothing. The question wasn't for her, and she had already been warned by one of the officers earlier that day that she was to let her daughter speak for herself. Whether Joanne would do so was yet to be seen. The poor girl was clearly terrified.

'We'd like to take a little look at you, Joanne, to make sure everything's okay. Would that be all right?'

The girl appeared to suck air between her teeth before leaning forward, and the doctor had little chance to react when she was sick across the tiled floor. Jackie left the room to fetch tissues and a glass of water. She too felt nauseous, distressed at the thought of the post-mortem examination she knew was being carried out on Joanne's baby that afternoon.

As she returned to the room, DI Peter Greene approached

her. He reached for her arm and ushered her into an empty interview room before closing the door behind him.

'You never told me you knew the boy's mother.'

Jackie bit her lip. She had known this would be an issue if anyone was to find out, and she had hoped to keep it so that no one did. The last person she had wanted to know was Peter, though she should have realised he would make the link. Her friendship with Lynne Parker didn't affect her professional ability, and she wouldn't let it sway her judgement. She was prepared to deal with the facts in the same way everyone else was doing. Yet despite her resolution to remain impartial, what had happened to Nathaniel had crushed her. She wished desperately she could undo it all somehow. Lynne would be devastated to know that Jackie was in the same building as the family involved in his death.

'I'm sorry,' was all she could manage.

'You're her friend, for Christ's sake. It's a murder investigation.'

She couldn't look at him. She felt her eyes fill at the thought of Nathaniel and what had been done to him. Joanne's father and brother had apparently beaten him so badly that Lynne had barely recognised him when she'd been taken to identify his body. How was she going to recover from this? How did anyone get over the tragedy of losing a child?

'I'm not with the police, though,' she said quietly, desperate to defend herself. 'I'm just here to oversee the examination.'

'You're too close to this, Jackie,' he said, taking a step towards her and putting a hand on her arm. 'I'm assuming you knew the boy well too?'

She nodded. She had known the Parker family for a number of years now, since before Nathaniel's sister had been born. Lynne had been a good friend to her, someone she had trusted with the details of her marriage. Someone she had spoken to about her feelings for Peter.

'Are you going to tell anyone?' she asked.

He sighed and raised his eyes to the ceiling. 'No. But I could get in a lot of trouble if anyone finds out I've lied for you.'

Jackie nodded her gratitude. Her career meant everything to her. Even as a child, all she had ever wanted to do was care for others. She hoped to move into midwifery one day, when the time was right, but should anyone find out that she had withheld information from the police, she knew she would never get the chance. She would never be employed by a health board again.

'Thank you,' she said quietly.

'I don't want you to thank me. Just show me I'm not making a massive error of judgement here, please.' Peter sighed. 'Are you okay?'

She shook her head. She felt her eyes fill with tears, trying desperately to keep them from view. He was right: it was all too close to home. He said nothing, but moved his hand to hers for a moment.

'What's going to happen to Joanne?' she asked. 'Will she face prosecution for the burial?'

'I doubt it,' Peter said. 'It wouldn't be in the public interest to punish her any further. The poor girl's been through enough.'

'I drove by the house this morning. There are already obscenities spray-painted on the window.'

'News travels fast, unfortunately.'

Jackie wondered what might happen to the family now, in the aftermath of what had happened. The community was a small and relatively close-knit one; it wouldn't be long before people found out what had taken place there as a prelude to Nathaniel's murder. *Murder.* The word reverberated in her brain, unable to fix itself to any sense of reality. It was a barbaric act of violence, premeditated and brutal. Joanne and Elizabeth Mansfield might not have been present during the attack, but Jackie knew how people's minds worked, and how easily judgement fell. They would be considered no better than Jamie and Trevor.

'I'd better get back,' she said, turning away.

Back in the room where Joanne and her mother were waiting, she handed the glass of water to the girl, who took it without acknowledging her.

'Joanne has agreed to the examination,' Dr Vine told her. 'We'll make a start in a moment.'

Jackie waited as the girl drained the glass of water. A screen was pulled across the room so that she could undress and prepare herself on the bed. The examination passed without a word from anyone other than the doctor, and when it was over, Joanne dressed herself silently. She hadn't spoken to a single person since she had been there, not even her mother. Jackie couldn't imagine how her young life was ever going to move on from what had happened.

She needed to see Lynne, but what was she going to say to her? There were no words that could come close to offering any kind of comfort to her and Malcolm, and then there was Melissa to consider. How was any of what had happened going to be explained to a child just nine years old?

Peter's words replayed as she left the police station. *Just show me I'm not making a massive error of judgement here.* Jackie had gone home that day knowing that she was indebted to him. Almost thirty years later, he would seek her out for the return of the favour.

FORTY-THREE

THE MOTHER

By the time Lauren made it to the front door, the ambulance was pulling up at the kerbside. She'd managed to pull on a pair of trousers, though the effort of this small and everyday task had left her exhausted. She felt weak and dizzy and had lost too much blood, but she was not going to give in to the pain this time, not while her daughter needed her. Melissa was deranged, beside herself with desire for revenge, but she wasn't a monster. It was Joanne she wanted to hurt, not the child. She wouldn't do anything to harm a newborn baby, would she?

Yet wouldn't that be the worst of ways – the best of ways – in which to exact her revenge? She had been waiting for this moment. She had been waiting for the birth.

The paramedics who'd come expecting to find a woman in labour were now confronted with the news that they were dealing with the victim of a stabbing. Lauren's words spilled from her in a desperate muddle as she told them about her stolen daughter.

'Through there,' she said, gesturing to the hallway. 'Her name's Jackie. I can't find a pulse.'

The paramedic put a hand on her shoulder. 'Have you called the police?'

She hadn't. She had no idea what had happened to her phone; presumably Melissa had taken it at some point. 'Help me,' she pleaded. 'I just need to find my baby.'

The confused paramedic put out a call for police as his female colleague appeared from the other side of the ambulance. Moments later, a police car pulled into the street. It couldn't possibly have been in response to the call just made; it was too soon, the paramedic having only just ended the call. A uniformed officer got out from the driver's side before a second man emerged from the passenger seat. Lauren recognised him straight away. The man who had been at Jamie's funeral. The man who had been watching her outside her home. The Kuga driver.

'Lauren? We need you to come with us.'

'Who are you? Why have you been following me?'

'I'll explain in the car. Come on. I know where she's taken your baby.'

She had no choice but to trust the stranger. Whoever he was, he knew her. He'd been watching her for long enough.

One of the paramedics rushed out of the house to get something from the ambulance.

'Is she...?' the man asked, unable to finish the question.

'She's critical,' the paramedic told him. 'We need to get moving.'

When Lauren looked at the man beside her, she saw concern stamped on his face – and, she thought, guilt. Who was he to Jackie? she wondered. Whatever their relationship, Jackie had endangered herself to save Lauren. To save her baby.

'We need to get you to hospital too,' the paramedic said.

'I'm fine. I just need to find my baby.'

The man beside her flashed an ID card at the paramedic.

'I'll take care of her. Please... just make sure Jackie pulls through.'

He guided Lauren to the car as the paramedic rushed back into the building.

'Melissa hired a car,' he explained, as Lauren put on her seat belt. She winced in pain. She suspected she needed stitches, but it would have to wait. 'We've got the registration,' the man continued, watching her with concern. 'We got her location?' he asked the officer in the driving seat.

The man nodded. 'They're in pursuit.'

As the sound of the car's siren filled the air around them, Lauren felt sick. Wherever Melissa was now, her child was with her, unclothed and unfed, completely vulnerable and at the mercy of a woman who had no concept of the notion. Did Melissa have a car seat? The woman was deranged with vengeance – she wouldn't care about the baby's safety. Lauren's mind drew images of her daughter flung into the footwell of a speeding car, and her body responded to the thought with a burst of pain that shot through her groin.

The driver spoke into his radio, but the words were a blur behind the noise of Lauren's fear.

'My name's Peter Greene,' the man said, putting a hand on her arm. 'I'm a former detective. I worked on the Nathaniel Parker murder case and I've been following Melissa Parker for a number of years now. Officers are tracking her. We're going to get your baby back safely.'

He was making a promise for which there was no guarantee. No one could possibly know what might happen in the next minutes or hours. Perhaps they were already too late.

Lauren looked down. Blood stained the front of her trousers. She should have felt pain, but fear overrode all else.

'I've worked as a private investigator since I retired from the police,' Peter continued, and Lauren wondered whether he was talking to try to distract her from the horrors that filled her mind. 'The last case I worked on while still a detective was the death of a young woman called Becky Hargreaves. She drowned in a bath at a house party. Melissa Parker was one of her housemates. She wasn't the first of Melissa's friends to have died an accidental death. Twenty years ago, just before she left her parents' house, a boy she'd been briefly involved with drowned after falling into a river after a night out. Melissa was investigated at the time, but there was no evidence strong enough to suggest she'd been involved. I was never convinced. I still think she was responsible for both deaths.'

'She killed my brother,' Lauren said quietly. 'She told me so while I was giving birth. The timing of the confession seemed to give her some sick satisfaction.'

'I am so sorry. I suspected she might have been involved. I knew she'd been to his flat, but the police think it was an accidental overdose.'

'Jamie was a mess. It wouldn't have been difficult for her to hide the crime. You were at the funeral. Why?'

'I thought she might show up. It seemed the kind of arrogant thing she would do.'

They fell silent as a voice came through on the radio. Lauren heard the words 'vehicle tyre deflation rounds deployed', though they meant nothing to her. She felt nerves pulsing through her stomach.

'They've shot out the tyres,' Peter explained.

She looked out of the window. She had no idea where they now were. Cars and buses moved aside to let them pass as the siren continued to blare, piercing the morning air. There was shouting through the radio, voices muffled by movement as whatever was happening at the other end of the link played out beyond their sight. Then the officer driving met a roadblock manned by uniformed police, through which he was allowed to pass. They were here, Lauren thought. Her daughter was on this road. So was Melissa.

Through the windscreen, she saw a police car stopped in the middle of the road. Beyond it, another car was also stationary. Melissa. The back tyres were flattened, and two armed officers were now standing within metres of the vehicle.

Lauren pushed open the door as soon as the car stopped.

'Stay back,' Peter warned her. 'We don't know whether she's armed.'

They were on a residential street, tree-lined and affluent. In a big bay window opposite, a little girl was watching the scene unfolding outside. She couldn't have been more than six years old, and Lauren wished she could cover her eyes and keep her innocence protected. A moment later, a figure appeared behind the child. She was moved from the window, the curtains pulled shut.

'Step out from the vehicle!'

The first of the armed officers moved closer to the car. The empty street was bathed for a moment in a paralysed silence, then the driver's door opened. Lauren saw a pair of jeans, a hooded sweater. Melissa emerged from the car with a bundle in her arms: Lauren's daughter, still wrapped in the towel Melissa had taken from the flat. She was using the baby as a shield, she thought. The officer raised his weapon.

The scream that built inside her had nowhere to go, her voice rendered mute with the horror of the scene that was unfolding.

She felt Peter's hand on her arm. 'Let them do their job.'

But no one seemed to be doing anything. Mere moments must have passed, but to Lauren it felt that a lifetime had passed.

'Bring the baby to me, Melissa,' the officer said, his voice calm and measured.

Why wasn't the baby crying? Newborn babies cried. She must have been starving, wondering where her mother was, so why wasn't there a sound? Lauren looked at the bundle held close to Melissa's chest. The woman was suffocating her.

'Bring the baby to me,' the officer repeated, but his words were again met with no response from Melissa. She held the officer's eye, a defiance in her face that was terrifying. There was no remorse in her expression, and when she turned to look at Lauren, she saw an emptiness that chilled her to the core. Melissa looked dead behind the eyes, removed from the situation and everything around her.

She broke free from Peter's grip and grimaced in pain as she ran towards her child. She felt dizzy with blood loss, her vision impaired by pain and tears. 'Give her to me, Melissa,' she said, stopping a few feet from the other woman and holding out her hands. 'Hurting her won't bring Nathaniel back.'

'Don't speak his name,' Melissa said through gritted teeth. 'Don't you ever speak his name again.'

An accusation rang through Lauren's head, but she held it back, saving it where it had been suppressed for all these years. *He wasn't who you think he was.* If she spoke the words now, she would never be able to retract them. Her daughter would pay the price for them.

'Please,' she said, still clinging to the hope that a last sliver of humanity remained embedded somewhere within Melissa's conscience. 'Don't do this.'

Melissa moved, and Lauren lunged to grab her baby. A single shot rang out in the silent street.

The air left Lauren's lungs. She watched as Melissa fell to the side, the bullet embedded in her lower leg, and felt her heart stop as she saw her daughter slip from her hands. She heard her own scream as though she was hearing the sound of someone else's voice from underwater.

Then somehow her baby was in the arms of the other officer, the two men having worked silently together to free her from Melissa's clutches as Lauren distracted her. He held her out to Lauren, and with her baby against her chest, she finally released a torrent of tears. There was shouting as Melissa was handcuffed, the street suddenly awash with officers and paramedics. Lauren felt a hand on her arm as she was guided to an ambulance, but all she could see was her daughter.

'Is she okay?' she asked the female paramedic waiting by the ambulance.

'We'll check her over, but do you want to give her a feed first? Poor thing's probably starving.'

Lauren got into the ambulance, and the paramedic closed the door to give her privacy. Outside, she heard Melissa's protests as she was taken away by the police. It was over, she thought. Finally, it was all over.

The baby took to her breast and fed until she fell asleep. Lauren held her in the curve of her arm and watched her chest rise and fall beneath the towel in which she was wrapped. She didn't look like a Sophia. The name had been a possibility, though she hadn't been set on anything. Now, looking at her sleeping face, a name came to her instantly.

She took the girl's tiny hand between her fingers and gently rubbed her palm, the pain that coursed through her body for the moment forgotten. 'Hello, Faith,' she managed to say. 'It's lovely to meet you at last.' And as she looked up at the paramedic getting into the back of the ambulance, Lauren passed out.

FORTY-FOUR

THE MIDWIFE

The weather had warmed over the past week, and Jackie was grateful to finally be out of hospital, though she knew the flat would not be home for much longer. Returning to the place had felt like taking a step backwards into a life she hadn't wanted to return to, one that in so many ways had been forced upon her through a sense of obligation and debt. Despite everything that had happened, she had no regrets. She had been enlisted to help save a life – possibly two – and she had done what she had set out to.

She got off the bus and made her way on foot to the park. Though the weather was lovely, the place was quiet; it was a Wednesday afternoon, and the children who would fill the playground at the weekend were all at school, their parents moving through the motions of their daily lives. Jackie wondered what daily life was like now for Lauren, her world having shifted into a routine of feeds and naps, wrapped in those first couple of months of exhaustion and wonderment. She felt a familiar pang in her chest, though it was lessened now, bearable.

She and Lauren hadn't seen each other since the morning of the delivery. Jackie remembered holding the baby close to her chest and pleading with Melissa to change her mind; after that, all she could recall was a searing pain that had felt like dying. She had woken up in hospital, her mind blanked of the period between then and now, grateful for the glare of the strip lighting and the intermittent bleeping of the machines that surrounded her. Thankful to be alive.

But she'd had no idea what had happened to the baby. Events of that morning came rushing back in a flurry of memory: the knife, the child, the world fading into a blackness she had felt at the time would be final. Had Melissa taken Lauren's daughter? Was she capable of harming a newborn child? Peter had visited later that day. Relief had flooded her with the news that both Lauren and the baby were safe and well. All the lies she'd had to tell and all the deceit she'd been guilty of were worth it. The pain of her injury had a purpose.

Melissa was in custody facing trial on multiple charges: three of murder, one of attempted murder and one of abduction. Once she'd been caught, she'd apparently been keen to make sure the police were aware of all her crimes. Peter had predicted this might happen, having encountered criminals like her before, the kind who once backed into a corner wore their sins as badges of honour, basking in the notoriety that their crimes might now earn them. The story had been plastered across the news, and Lauren's anonymity had been decimated by the media. She had likely known that the truth of her past would one day catch up with her, though it had happened in the worst of ways. Jackie hoped she would encounter only what she deserved: sympathy and kindness.

In the park, her heart fluttered at the sight of Lauren sitting on a bench, the pram beside her. She had lost a lot of weight, too much for someone who had only recently given birth. Jackie hoped she was looking after herself.

Lauren looked up and saw her approaching.

'Thanks for agreeing to meet me,' Jackie said. She stood

awkwardly for a moment, not knowing whether she should sit or keep a distance between them. Lauren's silence spoke more than any words might have: she was still wary of her, and Jackie couldn't blame her for that.

'How have you been?'

'Okay. Adjusting.'

Jackie nodded. The pram was turned away from her so that the hood kept the baby hidden. 'Can I take a look?'

Lauren nodded.

Jackie stepped around the pram and peered in at the baby. She was sleeping beneath a pink blanket, her tiny hands curled into little fists either side of her head. 'She's perfect.'

'Why did you do it?' Lauren asked suddenly. 'Why did you put us in so much danger? There must have been another way.'

Jackie bit her lip and moved back around the pram, taking a seat next to Lauren. She winced as she sat, the pain from her healing injury still yet to leave her. 'If there had been any other way, believe me, I would have taken it. Peter contacted me to tell me about Melissa. He'd been following her for a while, and he knew that she'd found you. She knew where you'd been for your IVF treatment. We don't know how,' she added, seeing Lauren's reaction, 'but we could only assume that you'd become an obsession for her. In much the same way Melissa was for Peter, I suppose. He was convinced she would try to hurt you both; it was the perfect opportunity for revenge. He knew I'd been working in London for a while, and he asked for my help. I got a transfer to Pinewood Hospital once he found out that that was where you were a patient. We were trying to keep you safe, although I know it can't have felt that way.'

'You exposed me to so much danger. You encouraged me to meet her knowing all the time who she was and everything that had happened. She might have done anything.'

'I know,' Jackie admitted. 'There were so many times I was far from comfortable with what I was doing. But I trusted Peter, and I was right to. We were trying to protect you, to protect Faith. Those sessions at the community centre... I had to have Melissa believe I was on her side. She thought I was going to help her.'

Jackie had known that introducing Melissa as Amber to Lauren had been a risky thing to do, but being able to control their meetings seemed less of a danger than allowing Melissa to act alone. There had also still been a part of her that hadn't wanted to believe Peter. Perhaps she could prove him wrong. Maybe she could talk Melissa down, try to persuade her that Lauren had been as much a victim as she had. Perhaps she could help both women. But she could never have changed Melissa's mind, something she had realised too late.

'She thought you were going to help her to do what?'

Jackie closed her eyes. Lauren knew the answer to her own question, and neither of them really wanted to be reminded of what Melissa's plans had been for Lauren and her child. 'I am so, so sorry. I should never have brought the two of you together, but my hands were tied. The group was her idea. If I'd refused to go ahead with it, she would have started to doubt me. Once she'd found out I was trying to protect you rather than help her, God only knows what she would have done.'

The more she talked, the more Jackie felt herself digging a hole she might never be able to get herself out of. She fell silent, allowing Lauren time to absorb her words and interpret them in whatever way she felt suitable.

'There were some strange exchanges between the two of you, I only realised that recently,' Lauren said. 'At that first meeting, when you were talking about yoga classes and whatever, you said something about it being important to be around people. You were trying to warn me even then, weren't you?'

'Not consciously, perhaps,' Jackie admitted. 'But your safety was always my priority. Yours and Faith's.'

'You already knew me, didn't you? You'd met me long before that day at the hospital.'

'I was at the police station the day you were examined by the doctor. I was a nurse at the time, before I moved into midwifery. There always have to be two people present for any examination, and yours was such a sensitive case, with you being so young. You don't remember me because you never saw me. I don't think you looked at a single person that day. In all my years, I've never seen anyone look as scared as you did. Skinny little slip of a thing, you were. Just a child. But I knew your fear wasn't what everyone else thought it was. It was your father you were terrified of, wasn't it?'

Lauren didn't answer. Jackie suspected she didn't need to. She was right: Joanne had feared her father's temper, and in the aftermath of Nathaniel's death, she must have realised she'd been right to. But Lauren wasn't there to talk about her relationship with her parents. There were answers she needed from Jackie, too many things she still didn't understand and probably believed she could never forgive.

There was a tiny cry from the pram; the baby had woken. Jackie watched as Lauren lifted her tenderly from where she'd been sleeping. She held her to her chest and wrapped the blanket around her, swaying gently as she soothed her.

'Why did you turn full circle on the idea of a home birth? When Melissa first mentioned it at the group meeting, you seemed annoyed with her. But then you changed your mind. You actively encouraged it. You responded with anger when I rejected the idea. Didn't you think I would have been safer at the hospital, where we would have been around more people?'

'Given everything we knew Melissa to be capable of, Peter and I thought you'd be safer at home, where he'd be able to keep watch on the house. Hospitals are big and busy places, even on the maternity wards.' Jackie swallowed nervously. 'Mistakes get made,' she admitted, thinking of her own recent error with the drug administration. 'And Melissa is smart and unnervingly convincing. She'd have found her chance to get to you, one way or another.'

'So where was he?' Lauren asked. 'How did Melissa manage to get to the flat that night?'

'Peter's daughter had needed him. She called that afternoon – there was some sort of emergency. He went to her. It was my fault... I thought there was still time. He was on his way back when I'd called him.'

Lauren sat down on the bench, but as soon as she did, Faith started to cry. She stood back up, and the baby's tears instantly subsided. 'I guess I'm going to be spending a lot of time on my feet,' she said with a smile. It quickly fell from her face as her thoughts returned to Melissa. 'How did you know the family?'

Jackie felt as though she was being interrogated, but she had gone there expecting as much. Lauren deserved the truth. 'Melissa's mother, Lynne, was a friend of mine. We'd met through a community group at the church, and I knew the family well. She'd just found out she was pregnant with Melissa at the time. After Nathaniel's death, nobody antici-pated her suicide, although in hindsight I felt we should have. Nathaniel was her world. Her husband could never get over the fact that she had left her daughter when she'd needed her most, and I think that was instilled in Melissa, that sense that her mother had abandoned her. Lynne must have felt totally desperate. Stop it,' she added, seeing the expression of dismay that had fixed itself upon Lauren's face. 'None of it was your fault. You weren't responsible for what your father and brother did.'

Lauren's eyes filled with tears. 'I'm so sorry,' she said. 'About Nathaniel... his mother... everything.'

Jackie stood and went to her. 'Don't do this to yourself. You have nothing to apologise for.' She smiled as Faith turned her head to look at her. The baby's eyes were a brilliant blue. 'Hello, you.' She reached to take the baby's tiny fingers in her own. 'I think someone's been here before. She's a wise one.'

Her words brought a silence that felt suffocating.

'Do you want to hold her?' Lauren asked eventually.

It was the last thing Jackie had expected. She had thought Lauren wouldn't want her anywhere near either of them, but as the other woman held Faith towards her, it seemed that perhaps she was beginning to forgive her. She hadn't realised until that moment just how much she needed it and how much it meant to her.

She took the baby gently and held her in her arms, swaying to soothe her in the same way Lauren had.

'What will you do now?' Lauren asked. 'Are you going to stay at the hospital?'

Jackie sighed. She'd had plenty of time to consider her future, though she still hadn't resolved upon a plan. The investigation into her deceit at the hospital was still ongoing; although she had technically broken no rules, her prior links to Lauren and the methods she'd used to get close to her were now widely known, and the ethics surrounding her conduct were under consideration. There was a chance she would be struck off. Her best intentions had been taken into consideration as mitigating circumstances, but whether they would be enough was yet to be seen.

'I'll probably do what I was planning to do before Peter contacted me. Retirement. I fancy a bit of time abroad. Maybe Portugal.'

'You've earned it. You should do it. And what about Peter?'

'Peter's gone back to his family in Hampshire. Now that Melissa is where she belongs, his work is finally done.'

'You two aren't...'

Jackie shook her head. 'We served a purpose. There's too much water under the bridge, as they say.' She handed the baby back to her mother. 'Do you forgive me?'

There was a lengthy silence before Lauren answered. 'Even this morning, I wasn't sure I could ever forgive you for the danger you'd exposed us both to. I think I've worked my way through every emotion that exists over the past month – anger, resentment, sadness. Gratitude. But I know you're right about Melissa – she would have found a way to reach me one way or another. I know you had our best interests at heart.' She paused to look at her daughter, who gazed up at her wide-eyed. 'In a different version of events, one where you weren't there, perhaps neither of us would be here. So the short answer is yes. I forgive you.'

Relief flooded her. Both of them would now finally be able to move on with their lives. 'What happened all those years ago wasn't your fault,' she said. 'You were just a child. Stillbirth is an awful thing, the cruellest of things, but telling someone about your baby wouldn't have saved her, Lauren, even had you known you were pregnant.'

She reached out to put a hand over Lauren's. When Lauren's eyes met hers, they were filled with tears.

'There's something else I've never told anyone,' she said. 'Something my mother told me just before she died, about that night. The baby wasn't stillborn. My mother smothered her.'

FORTY-FIVE

THE MOTHER

The conversation she'd had with Jackie in the park had been a cathartic process, one she hoped might enable her to move on from the horrors of the past few months. She and Jackie would probably never see one another again, and perhaps that was the best thing for both of them. Maybe now they would both be able to start over, freed from the pasts that had kept them bound with guilt and regret.

Finally telling someone about her mother's confession had been a weight lifted, one she had carried alone for far too long. The admission had brought with it a tirade of emotions: anger, betrayal, sadness, resentment. Lauren had remained loyal to her mother during their multitude of moves from place to place, and in Elizabeth's final years, she had cared for her throughout her illness. She had believed her as much a victim of her husband's tyrannical rule over the house as she and Jamie had been. Her efforts had been rewarded with a confession that had broken her anew, and she had felt herself duped into loyalty to a woman who had betrayed her in the very worst of ways, her violence no different to that of her brother and father.

There had been a post-mortem on the baby, which had

concluded that she had died during childbirth due to a lack of oxygen. Had it stated otherwise, the truth of what Elizabeth Mansfield had done might have been revealed at the time. The note that had been wrapped around the brick had confirmed the legacy Joanne's mother had left her: she was condemned to life on the run. Her mother had repeatedly reminded her that the baby needn't have died had she only told someone of her pregnancy. The house was unequipped for a delivery; her mother had been unprepared. All of it was lies. Her child had lived, yet she hadn't known it until years later. And there was only so long someone could run from themselves.

There was one truth Lauren couldn't offer Jackie. Nathaniel had been like a nephew to the woman, and what good would come of staining her memory of him now? Joanne's parents had been right in their accusation: Nathaniel *had* raped her. She had never told them this, still unsure even years later that that was what had happened. She had never told anyone, scared of the repercussions and the judgement. She had fancied him. She had gone to meet him wearing an outfit her father would never have allowed her to wear had he known; she had led him on and she had got what she deserved. She had buried the secret deep within her, refusing to admit what had happened that night. But despite everything, she never believed that what her father and brother had done to him was justified. One sin couldn't be erased with another.

There was one person to whom Lauren still owed the truth. She hadn't seen Karim since before Faith's birth. He had sent her flowers, and a beautiful hand-stitched blanket embroidered with the baby's name. He had called and messaged her, and they had talked over the phone, but any time he'd suggested meeting up, Lauren had always found an excuse not to: health visitor appointments or hospital check-ups. She wanted to see him, but she didn't know where she might begin in explaining everything that had happened or who she really was.

She hadn't heard from him in over a week before she called
him to invite him over. To her surprise, he accepted the invitation, and the following day he arrived at the flat with a box of
chocolates and a soft toy. He followed her into the living room,
where Faith was sleeping in a Moses basket.

'How are you feeling?'

'Okay. We're doing well.'

He kept a respectful distance from the crib, waiting for her
to tell him that he could take a look. Would he even want to?
she wondered. Faith would bring back a flood of memories that
might be too painful for him to face.

'I read about that woman. I'm so sorry you went through all
that alone, Lauren.'

'I wasn't alone, not really. There was the midwife.'

Until now, she hadn't spoken to Karim about the links that
bound her and Melissa. Melissa's picture had appeared in the
local news, and he knew that she was responsible for the fire
and the brick through the window, but Lauren had not yet
ventured into the details of their shared past, fearful that once
the truth was out, he would no longer want to know her. It was
this that made her realise how close they had inadvertently
grown. She didn't want to leave London, and she didn't want to
leave him. But she was damaged, and it wasn't his responsibility
to repair her. That was something she was going to have to do
herself.

'Would you like a cup of tea?' she asked.

Karim followed her into the kitchen and waited in the
doorway while she put the kettle on. 'I wish you'd felt you could
talk to me.'

'I wouldn't have known where to begin,' she told him, her
back still turned to him. 'I'd never talked to anyone about what
happened.'

She poured boiling water into two mugs and swirled the tea
bags around with a spoon.

'Well, if you'd like to talk now, I want to listen.'

Lauren finished making the tea and handed him a mug. They went back into the living room and sat next to each other on the sofa.

'My real name is Joanne Mansfield. When I was fourteen years old, I was raped by a boy from my school. I got pregnant, but I didn't know I was pregnant until the night the baby was born. I didn't put on much weight, I didn't have any symptoms. I felt fine. Normal. I hadn't been having periods for very long so there was nothing unusual when they didn't show up. I started to have these stomach pains, and I went into labour while I was doing my homework. I gave birth in the bathroom. My mother helped with the delivery, though she didn't really speak to me during it. It all happened quickly, and I never saw the baby. Not until...'

She stopped talking. At her side, Karim sat silently, waiting until she was ready to continue. He must have known what came next – or at least he knew the version that everyone else had thought they'd known. Her story was available to find for anyone who knew it could be searched for.

'She was in a shoebox when I saw her,' she continued, trying to force away the image that had stayed with her for all those years, still so clear it was as though it had happened just the day before. 'I cut a blanket to put in the box because there was nothing else small enough to fit. I kept telling my mother that we should tell someone, but she just kept saying that I'd be in too much trouble. She told me the police would come and that they'd think I'd killed the baby. I was terrified. She kept saying that I should have told someone I was pregnant. She didn't believe I hadn't known. She said that if I'd told someone, the baby would have lived. That I'd killed her. She would have lived if it wasn't for me.'

Karim's hand slid into hers, though he remained silent. She noticed the band of skin indented by a wedding ring that had long since been removed. Everyone wore their tragedies in some form, some people better able to recognise the signs.

'The press reported a rape allegation, though I never said that Nathaniel had raped me. I never said it to my parents and I never said it to the police. I didn't speak to the police; my mother did all the talking. I didn't want to acknowledge what had happened – a kind of self-preservation, I suppose. She hadn't wanted anyone to find out about the baby, but my father and brother went looking for Nathaniel that night. They beat him and left him in the playground at the local park, where a group of kids from our school found him. I think my parents probably convinced themselves that the lie they'd told about him was true, to make themselves feel better about what they were guilty of; that his alleged crime somehow cancelled theirs. It wouldn't have made it any less abhorrent had they known the truth. Less than a fortnight after his death, Nathaniel's mother took her own life. Her daughter, Melissa, found her hanging from the washing line in the garden. She was nine years old at the time.'

Lauren felt Karim's reaction in the flinch of his hand in hers. Despite everything that had happened and all Melissa was responsible for, Lauren still couldn't bring herself to hate her, in the same way that she had never truly been able to hate her brother.

'Our home was targeted, spray paint across the doors and a brick through the window. For a while my mother and I were given police protection. We moved away, changed our names, started a new life. You can't ever run away, though, not really. The past travels with you.'

And then she told Karim what she had told Jackie at the park, something she'd never been able to tell anyone until that week. Karim sat silently as he listened, not speaking until Lauren had finished everything she wanted to say.

'I am so sorry. Everything you've been through, I just can't even begin to imagine it.'

'When you talked about Zarah, I couldn't tell you how much we had in common. I lost a daughter too, although the circumstances were very different.' She finished her tea before reaching to put the empty mug on the coffee table beside the sofa. 'You don't hate me?'

'Hate you?'

'For lying about who I am.'

Karim's fingers tightened around hers. 'I could never hate you.'

They were interrupted by a soft cry from the crib. Lauren got up to see to Faith, whose blue eyes were searching for her mother. She felt Karim at her shoulder as she reached down to pick up the baby. She nestled her into the curve of her arm before turning to him.

'She's beautiful,' he said.

'Would you like to hold her?'

There was a moment of hesitation, and Lauren feared she had pushed things too far too quickly. She wondered whether Karim had held a baby since Zarah's death.

Then he reached to her, and Lauren placed Faith in his hands, his strong arm curving around her back to cradle her. 'Look at you,' he said, taking the little girl's fingers in his own. 'You're perfect.'

His eyes moved from the baby to fix on Lauren.

'Why London?' he asked. 'What brought you here?'

'I spent years moving from place to place, sharing houses with people who were little more than strangers. London was the first place I felt lost, properly, for the first time. I could be anyone here, so I decided to stay. It's the only place in almost thirty years I've felt I've ever really been able to call home.'

'So don't leave.' The words came quickly, as though once they were spoken he wouldn't be able to take them back. 'Stay.'

'What do you mean?'

'Stay in London. I don't want you to leave – either of you.'

'I can't afford to stay,' Lauren said honestly. 'And after everything that's happened...'

'Then let's go somewhere else together.'

She laughed. The suggestion was so spontaneous, something her life had never allowed her to be.

'Don't think this is all for you,' Karim said as he passed Faith back to her. 'I'm being selfish here too. I've never felt I deserved a second chance, but maybe that isn't true. Perhaps I can do better this time. Get things right.'

Lauren looked from Faith to Karim. 'You're being serious, aren't you?'

'Absolutely. I can still run the business remotely, and I can develop it wherever we end up. Your skills are transferable – you'll find another job easily. I don't need an answer now, I just want you to think about it. This could be a fresh start for both of us. I know it's early days, but if we managed to get through the past few months together, we can get through anything.'

Lauren listened to his words with a sense of disbelief and possibility, waiting for a laugh or a wagged finger to chide her for being so gullible. Neither came. For so long she had lived in the shadow of the past, fearful of a future that seemed desolate and alien. It had been like living in limbo, never knowing from one day to the next how long she would be able to keep running before the next move became inevitable. She had lived a lie for almost three decades, fleeing from the terrible secret she had kept hidden. Hiding from who she was and from a past for which she had blamed herself for too long. She couldn't do it any more. She didn't want to. And for the first time ever, perhaps she didn't have to.

A LETTER FROM VICTORIA

Dear Reader,

Thank you so much for choosing to read *The Midwife*. If you enjoyed it and would like to keep up to date with all my latest releases, just sign up at the following link. Your email address will never be shared, and you can unsubscribe at any time.

www.bookouture.com/victoria-jenkins

The Midwife was one of those stories that took on a life of its own, and by midway through writing, it only vaguely resembled the synopsis I had sent to my editor. The idea was simple: a pregnant woman is targeted by the midwife who is to deliver her baby, with the two women's pasts intertwined. Jackie Franklin's character was initially planned to be a sinister one, though there was always the intention that an 'is she, isn't she?' doubt would hang over her. As the story progressed and her interactions with Lauren developed, so did my ideas of who and what she was. I came to see her only as inherently good – the 'guardian angel' that a young Melissa had perceived her to be.

The idea for Lauren's past came after reading about an American teenager who buried her stillborn child in her parents' garden. The comments section demonstrated the contrast in response to the girl's situation and her reaction to it. The case provoked a series of questions. How does someone move on from a tragedy such as this? Can someone ever 'escape' their past? How might this person approach the prospect of parenthood later on in life? Lauren's loss brought about the idea for Jackie's, and her history of recurrent miscarriages. Midwifery must bring at times harrowing experiences, but what of a woman who must cope with her own fertility issues while watching others' joy? In the end, Jackie and Lauren have more in common than either imagines, and I hope readers are able to find sympathy for both.

I hope you enjoyed *The Midwife*; if you did, I would be very grateful if you could write a review. I would love to hear what you think, and reviews really do make a difference in helping new readers to discover my books for the first time.

I love hearing from readers – you can get in touch through my Facebook page or on Twitter.

Thank you,

Victoria

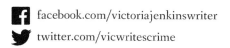

facebook.com/victoriajenkinswriter

twitter.com/vicwritescrime

ACKNOWLEDGEMENTS

Thank you to my editor, Helen Jenner, who fine-tunes my ramblings and endures my ongoing self-doubt, and as always to my agent, Anne Williams, my first reader and source of great support. Thank you to the team at Bookouture, who continue to make working with them an absolute pleasure, and especially to my publicist, Noelle Holten – thank you for sharing your knowledge and experience relating to probation officers.

Thank you to Stuart Gibson for answering my questions regarding police procedure, and thanks to Lucy Dauman for the help with London geography. Thanks also to Emma Tallon and Casey Kelleher, on hand as always for plotting advice and motivation – you are both sanity savers.

Thank you as always to my husband and my family, and thanks to my sister for being pregnant while I was writing this book – the timing was most convenient. As I write this, you are just over a week away from your due date, and I can't wait to welcome another little lady to our family's girl squad.

The most invaluable help in writing this book has come from Mark Smart, a lovely man and the brilliant midwife who delivered my first daughter. The biggest of thank yous for all your advice and guidance in making sure the midwifery references in this story are true to life, and thanks also to your colleague, Elaine Derrick. I have learned so much from you during this process, and can only wonder at what a rewarding, diverse and at times challenging career midwifery is. Mark, with the greatest of admiration and respect for all that you do, this book is for you.